I0778612

CAMDEN

MYSTERY CLUB

TRILOGY

ANNE HOTCHKIS

INK START MEDIA
265 Eastchester Dr Ste 133 #102
High Point NC 27262

TABLE OF CONTENTS

CODE BLUE AT THE QEH

BOOK 1

CAMDEN MYSTERY CLUB SERIES

CHAPTER 1

"Charlie! Call 911! I think Dad's taking a heart attack!" Trish's dad was clutching his upper body, falling to the floor, gasping for breath. Quickly Trish knelt beside her father loosening his shirt collar and began CPR on his chest. She was counting in her head; in the background she heard Charlie's urgent call to send an ambulance from the Queen Elizabeth Hospital.

Fifteen-year-old Trish Camden was shaking as she continued to count pressing down and releasing with the inhale and exhale of Dad's breathing. She had her first aid training and knew precisely how to handle the situation. Her brother, Charlie, calmly said, "The ambulance is on the way."

Trish assertively ordered her brother to write a message for their grandmother, Nancy. Charlie was excellent at writing messages. He knew that his grandmother who was at her bridge game would worry if no one was home. He wrote, "Nana, Trish and I have gone to the QEH with Dad. Don't worry. We'll be home later. I'll call with more information, Love Charlie." He laid the note on the kitchen table. Trish's performing non-stop

CPR kept her mind focused on her dad, RCMP Staff Sergeant Rob Camden.

Nancy moved in with her son and grandchildren at the time when Rob's wife, Grace, was killed tragically in an automobile accident. She had a very motherly influence on their lives which also gave purpose and meaning to her life. She was happy to be of service to the family, was a stay-at-home type of woman, cooked, maintained the household, and did the food shopping in Charlottetown once a week.

Just then the ambulance arrived and the Emergency Medical Service team took over. The pair of men in uniform laid the patient on the stretcher and praised Trish for her technique in first aid. Once the EMS turned on the siren and zoomed out of the yard heading for the hospital, Trish broke down and cried. "Now is not the time to cry. We have to follow them. Let's go," said Charlie. Trish wiped her nose on a paper towel and the two hopped into the old Toyota. Dad had a newer model from 2005 and donated it to Charlie on the condition that Charlie would drive Trish to some of her events and when Trish was able to drive she would have equal access to the car.

Charlie had patience in the emergency waiting room. He could read a newspaper or a magazine. Trish on the other hand was jittery, pacing the floor, watching people come and go. She felt as if it was taking too long. *Where was Dad anyway?* she thought. Finally a doctor approached them. "Are you two the Camdens?" he asked.

"Yes. How is he?"

"Your dad has had a heart attack and I've put two stents in his arteries. He will need plenty of rest. He will need to be monitored for a few days. When he gets home, he won't be able to drive for at least a month. I'm leaving it up to you to take care of him. Go home and come by tomorrow for a visit. He's resting now. I heard one of you was doing CPR on him. That saved his life."

"I did!" exclaimed Trish. "You did the right thing."

It was late. Before heading for home, Charlie made a call to Nana. She had been home for an hour and was worrying. Charlie said little on his cell phone except that they would be home soon and Dad was going to recover with lots of rest.

Home was a forest green bungalow on a dead- end street in the town of Cornwall. The property was spacious with its backyard bordering on the soccer field for Eliot Elementary School where both kids graduated in earlier years. This was the home that Rob and Grace had bought together several years before the children were born. At that time, Rob was a constable and Grace was a substitute teacher. Rob was quite a handyman; so with money being tight they purchased the bungalow partially finished and spent a couple of years finishing the basement and adding a garage. Like most young adults, they fulfilled their dreams of owning a home and had hopes of someday raising a family on this property which spurred them to build in Cornwall, a semi-rural setting, on the outskirts of Charlottetown.

The whole story came out at breakfast when Nana was making pancakes. Nancy was worried as any mother would be but she kept her feelings to herself as always. Trish ran to catch the bus and Charlie jumped into the car and headed for the university.

During the afternoon Trish got a text from Charlie that they would have to go to the hospital after supper, as he had a campus police meeting that couldn't be missed. Trish was agitated, wanting to get out of her boring math class and see Dad as soon as possible but all she texted back was "ok". Finally she put in her day and took the bus home to be greeted by the smell of roast beef and baked potatoes cooking in the oven.

"Nana, what ever would we do without you? Dinner smells delicious. Charlie is going to be late. He had a meeting. What time are we going to eat and did you see Dad today?"

"We will eat when Charlie gets home and I did go to the hospital and see Rob sitting up in bed. He was asking about you two. I presume you guys will go in this evening. The weather forecast is calling for freezing rain; so your brother will have to drive slowly," said Nancy.

After supper Charlie and Trish headed for the hospital under Nana's strict warning about road conditions. They tiptoed into their dad's room but saw him sitting up reading a newspaper. "Hi Dad," they said in unison.

"We miss you at home and the house feels so empty even though Nana is with us. It's just not the same when you're not there." They spent their visit talking about their passion for police detective work until visiting hours were almost over. "We'd better go now, Dad," said Trish. "See you tomorrow." She gave her dad a big hug and tears welled up in her eyes. Charlie gave his dad a hug too.

"Stay on the TransCanada Highway until you get to Cornwall. The roads could be slippery," said Dad.

As they left their dad's room, a stretcher was wheeled into the room next door, room 227.

Max Weldon had just come out of gallbladder surgery. A nurse and orderly moved him into his single room next to Rob Camden's. He was barely coherent but heard muffled voices as if kids were nearby. "See you tomorrow, Dad."

It was dark outside. The curtains were closed and he could hear sleet tapping at the windows. The nurse hooked up an intravenous bag which hung from a metal pole at his bedside. The orderly and nurse left him alone.

Max was feeling uncomfortable with the pain near his liver and the insertion site where the IV was put in his hand.

An orderly in pale blue scrubs entered. Max looked up and gasped at the person he recognized.

"This is for you, Max." The orderly inserted a needle into the stent in Max's vein, and quickly and quietly disappeared.

The job was complete. The orderly changed into street clothes in a nearby washroom and exited the hospital. Then got into a truck, guzzled gulps of whiskey and headed out of Charlottetown towards Cornwall.

Trish and Charlie stopped at the nurse's station to ask about their father when suddenly a code blue interrupted them. They were scared as an intern, a doctor and a couple of nurses rushed by them, but Trish and Charlie were so absorbed with thoughts of their dad they went back to his room and waited until all the commotion subsided and to make sure Dad was ok; then they left the hospital and headed home.

It was a cold, blustery night, a sleet storm in early November. A truck swerved back and forth across the road. "Watch out!" screamed Trish. Charlie reacted instantaneously, pulled the car to the right, spun out of control, and landed in the ditch. "Are you ok?" he asked.

"Yah," said Trish. "Who was that jerk? He didn't even stop!" Trish, the bubbly, assertive, outspoken sibling wore all of her emotions on her sleeve. She could charm anyone with her free spirit but at times she was a little on the hyper, over-reactive side.

The half-ton truck continued on its way down the highway veering from side to side. Trish twisted her petite figure around and managed a glimpse of the license plate on the back of the vehicle.

"Trish, if you can straighten the wheels, I'll get behind and push." The almost-six-foot-tall Charlie had a calm air about him. After a few tries, they managed to get the car out of the ditch and headed for home. It was a basic, three-bed bungalow with a finished rec room in the basement. Charlie and Trish moved downstairs when they started to hang out with friends and didn't want to disturb their dad's quiet space. The house looked very cold, dark, and lonely at night with only one small lamp on in Nana's bedroom. Nana was brought up in a frugal, Scottish home where extra lights were not left on, especially now with Dad in the hospital. Trish was still agitated about the near-miss collision. "It's a good thing I remembered that guy's license plate. I should report him," said Trish.

"Relax, Trish. Let it go. No harm done," said Charlie in his cool, rational voice. Charlie at age eighteen was a typical computer-age teenager; texting was preferable to using the phone. His cell phone kept him connected with his limited social life. Trish as well as owning a cell phone had her own mental computer, a photographic memory. Between the two of them they had solved some of the toughest cases their father had ever put to them.

Dad had asked them to phone to make sure they arrived home safely. The roads were dangerous; so they agreed to call. Charlie didn't want to be reprimanded for the accident even though it wasn't his fault, and so the two sleuths decided not to tell their father.

"We'll see you tomorrow, Dad. Good night," they said as they hung up the landline.

Charlie was so darn proud of his father that he wanted to become an RCMP officer just like him. Rob encouraged Charlie to take a university degree first; so Charlie enrolled at the University of Prince Edward Island (UPEI) in sociology.

Rob Camden thought about how his kids had grown so fast since Grace had died. It seemed as though it was yesterday and now he wondered what kind of drain he would be on his family and how he would adapt to the drastic change he was to make in his life. Rob hoped his mom, Nancy, would be with them for the long run.

Saturday was sunny and the sleet disappeared. Trish and Charlie bought a local newspaper and a Tim's coffee for Dad. They arrived just when Rob's surgeon, Dr. Sam Black, finished his examination. "Your dad is improving but you'll have to give him plenty of rest when he returns home," Dr. Black said. Once the surgeon left, Trish asked,

"Who was the code blue alert for last night, Dad? We saw lots of doctors and nurses in the room next door."

"A man died there. He came into my room yesterday before his operation. His name was Max Weldon and he was the manager at Scotiabank in town."

Trish and Charlie wanted to have a look around. Trish surveyed details of the hallway and approached the nurse's station to snoop. The nurse on duty had relieved the night-shift nurse and refused to engage in a conversation with a young girl. "Who was there?" Trish asked.

"I am not permitted to release any details at this time," she said sharply.

Trish and Charlie prattled about what they saw and began questioning their dad as to details about the man in room 227 and why a code blue alarm was sounded. "He walked into my room yesterday before his surgery. As I already told you, his name was Max Weldon and he was the bank manager at the Scotiabank downtown. We've known each other vaguely for years. Not close friends but acquaintances. Don't you two get any ideas about a murder investigation. This death might be due to complications from Max Weldon's surgery."

"Don't worry about us, Dad. We're going to have a look around. We'll be back to see you this afternoon. Take care and have a rest," said Trish.

"See you later, Dad," said Charlie.

Trish had an eerie sense she saw someone enter the public washroom last night when she and Charlie were standing at the nurse's station. Trish always reacted on her hunches and so she nudged Charlie to follow her into the public washroom across the hall from room 227.

Trish looked around the bathroom and didn't find much there. Then she checked the garbage can for clues. She quickly rummaged through the paper products. "Hey, look at all this," she said excitedly. She delved into the can and saw a pale blue orderly uniform, top and bottom, a brown, curly, short-hair wig which sent shivers up her spine as it looked just like her own hair style and color, a syringe and a pair of rubber surgical gloves. "I think we've hit the jackpot. We can't touch this stuff with our hands or we'll put our fingerprints on it. We'd better tell Dad, so that he can get Detective Freeman in here," said Trish.

"I bet this syringe has traces of a chemical that a lab would find is the cause of death of Mr. Weldon when the autopsy is done," said Charlie. Trish nodded. She was deep in thought about the orderly uniform. *When had she seen it and the curly, brown hair wig - coming into or out of Room 227? How tall was he? Her photographic memory was registering something that she hadn't quite captured. It gnawed at her brain but she couldn't recall it right now.*

Trish dismissed her uneasiness and focused on what her brother said.

"How are we going to find out what chemical was in that syringe?", Charlie asked. "I think Dad should call RCMP headquarters and speak to Sergeant Freeman. He'll know what we should do."

Trish and Charlie darted back into their dad's room. "Hey, Dad, Trish found something important in the public washroom across the hall."

"It looks like evidence that someone left in the garbage can last night after Max Weldon died. There is an orderly uniform, a brown wig, a syringe, and a pair of surgical gloves. We left the evidence there because it could lead to some kind of information that might be useful and you always taught us never to touch something with our bare hands that could be used to solve a crime. We didn't have rubber gloves," said Trish.

"That's good thinking, Trish. I had better call Coady Freeman, to check this out. Please pass me your phone, Charlie," said Rob Camden.

Sergeant Coady Freeman was a dedicated, slightly overweight, middle-aged, police officer and the father of fourteen-year-old twins, John and Josie. His kids were good friends with Trish. Coady Freeman, his wife, Barb, and Rob and kids would get together for family barbecues.

Sergeant Freeman arrived on the scene to collect exhibits from the bathroom where Trish had found the clues. He used rubber gloves as he collected the items. Freeman also kept the syringe separate from the other articles, so that he could send it to the lab himself.

Trish and Charlie took a coffee break in the cafeteria while Freeman was carefully assembling the evidence. "Let's head for the morgue," said Trish after gobbling up her cinnamon bun and gulping her chocolate milk.

"No, not yet." said Charlie. "We are not going to get anywhere by ourselves. We need to stay with Sgt. Freeman. Let's head back to unit 2 and stick with him."

"He's a good guy, maybe a little clumsy but an ok man. He's a little bit jittery too, don't you think, Charlie?" asked Trish.

"Yes, but he always gets his man," replied Charlie. "Let's keep him on our side. We may have more luck getting into the morgue if Dad can convince him to allow us to tag along."

It was half past eleven when the teenage detective team met Sgt. Freeman back at the unit. Sgt. Freeman was mystified as to how Rob Camden's kids found themselves in the middle of a murder investigation. His respect for their dad led him to follow up on their clues; besides it was always good to keep the boss' kids humored.

"As you know Rob, you called me to investigate a suspicious death. Your children have found some pertinent evidence." said the detective.

"Trish, Charlie, you've uncovered something significant here. Sergeant, would you please allow my kids to tag along with you?" asked Rob.

"If you insist."

"I think it would be a good experience for them," said Rob.

"Very well. Trish and Charlie, follow me," said Freeman.

The threesome headed up to the top level of the Charlottetown Hospital where the lab processed blood samples. Sergeant Freeman allowed Camden's sleuths to lead the way. He'd get there in his own time. Trish and Charlie kept a quick pace while the officer held the precious syringe. Sgt. Freeman passed the syringe to the technician. "I am investigating a homicide. The body is in the morgue right now. This syringe was found in proximity to the sight where the body was found. Can you detect the chemical that was in this syringe?" he asked.

"No, but I can tell you the blood sample taken from the body in the morgue had an overdose of morphine in it. I can take the syringe to have it analyzed but I must send it to the forensics lab in Halifax to have it examined."

"Fine," said the detective.

With that, Sgt. Freeman pushed the Camden kids out of the lab and took them to the side of the corridor. "Now we're going to the morgue." The detective and Camden sleuths took the elevator down to the basement of the hospital along a corridor to a remote area of the hospital. "Are you ready for this?" Freeman asked. "Excuse me for a minute as I must find a washroom. I'll be right back. Wait right here," as he pointed to a spot outside the door to the morgue. Quickly the detective rushed down the hall to a public washroom.

Trish, was wide-eyed and nervous. The door to the morgue was closed and a sign said, Do Not Open. Knock Before Entering. Trish whispered to Charlie, "Let's make our move and sneak in and hide before Freeman comes back." Charlie was hesitant but kept close to Trish as she stealthily slid into the morgue and hid behind a large white metal cabinet. Sgt. Freeman came out of the washroom and looked around for the Camden kids. *I'm not going to wait around for them to return,* he thought; so he ignored the Do Not Open sign and sauntered in. Dr. Mack Pathius glared. "Oh, I should have known it was you. Don't you ever read signs? I'm studying this body which arrived last night. Looks like an overdose. Look at his bluish-colored fingernails and lips and bluish coloration around his eyes. Could be morphine, don't you think?" suggested the coroner.

"The technician in the lab has checked blood samples and has confirmed this," said Freeman.

Morphine. of course. Where would it come from? Lots of it around a hospital, thought Trish. Trish and Charlie peeked around the cabinet to view the body of Max Weldon. They noticed the bluish fingernails and lips.

Trish was squeamish at the sight of the body. She wanted to get out of there fast. She grabbed Charlie by the arm and motioned him towards the doorway. "Let's go. We've seen enough," she whispered. She tugged at Charlie's arm and he gave in to her wishes.

Trish was going to be sick. The kids slipped out of the morgue unseen, and Trish headed to the nearest washroom where she vomited.

"That's all for now," said Mack Pathius to Freeman, "It appears to be a homicide. Someone injected a lethal dose of morphine into him probably at the IV site. No other needle marks. If the same substance in the syringe is in the blood sample, then I believe Sgt. Freeman you will be conducting a murder investigation. At this time I will show on the death certificate, death from unnatural causes."

Trish met up with Charlie and Sgt. Freeman in the hall. She was pale yet somewhat better. "I thought you two wanted to see the morgue. Well, I've been in there," said Freeman, "Stick together."

Charlie and Trish were in the lead as they headed down the corridor. Trish whispered, "It certainly looks as if we've got the poison analyzed. Morphine leaves one's fingernails and lips a bluish color. We don't need to wait a month for the tests on the syringe sent to Halifax."

Sgt. Freeman overheard Trish's comments. He caught up with them and said,

"Ok, kids. We know what killed the victim; you guys can leave the rest of the investigation to the RCMP. Go back to see your father now. Bye," said the sergeant in a dismissive tone.

Trish and Charlie were disappointed that their investigation with Freeman was over. They were the ones who had found the evidence in the first place. *We started the investigation; so why can't we tag along?* thought Trish.

The young detectives walked away and headed to the cafeteria for lunch and to discuss their next strategy.

"Let's make a list of suspects. We've always done this whenever we've played detective games with Dad," said Trish.

"Ok," said Charlie.

Trish's stomach was feeling better but she stuck with some basic foods like toast, jello, and tea. "Let's recall last night. The first people on the scene arrived after the code blue. They were the doctor, the nurses, and the intern. I'm pretty sure that's all I can recollect," said Trish matter-of-factly.

"Of course, Max's wife, that is, if he's married, could be a suspect, too," said Charlie.

"Let's check into the bank where Max Weldon worked. Dad said it was the Scotiabank downtown," said Trish. "We should also visit his neighborhood." Trish and Charlie left the cafeteria and went back to see their father.

"How are you, Dad? Charlie and I are heading out. Do you want us to bring you anything?" asked Trish. "Nana will be here this afternoon for a visit."

"I've got the newspaper and I'll have a rest. I'm glad you two are getting away from here for a while," said Dad. The team left the hospital and sprung into high-gear detective mode.

"Trish, I think it's time we had a meeting of the Camden Mystery Club," said Charlie. "It's Saturday; so why don't you get the club to meet this afternoon? You text the gang and ask them to meet at our place at two o'clock. Urgent." Charlie drove the car home as fast as he dared without breaking the speed limit. He and Trish pulled into the driveway. Trish received texts confirming that everyone would be there. When Charlie and Trish had news of a mystery, the club members were eager to get involved.

The CMC consisted of stout, chubby, sixteen-year- old, Paul, Freeman's twins, Josie, the studious, serious, fair-haired twin and her carefree, goofy, brother, John, and Trish. Charlie got involved as he was the oldest and only one who had a driver's license. He also kept the club as punctual as possible but Paul usually arrived a few minutes late. Today he came from one of his favorite Tim's with a doughnut in one hand, a coffee in his other, his Smart phone in his back pocket, and tried to ring the doorbell with his elbow. Trish greeted them as they came in through the front door and headed downstairs to the dingy, poorly-lit rec. room which they converted to a clubhouse. The room belonged to the club presently but in the past Trish and Charlie used to play mystery games there with their father back in the early millennium. As the years went on and the CMC was born, Rob Camden gave up on keeping the room tidy and organized; so he made a deal--keep the mess downstairs and don't let any case be confused with another one. At the present time, pictures were hung all over the walls which signified previous cases that were solved by well-known police officers.

The atmosphere was one of organized chaos. There was an old record player on a shelf in the corner that once belonged to Trish and Charlie's grandmother and which was accompanied by a box of old Beach Boys, Beatles, Monkeys, Carole King and Carly Simon albums. Surprisingly enough the old player still worked and Trish always played Beach Boys music at the onset of a CMC meeting. There was a television in an adjacent corner which was at least ten years old but was fine for playing video games. The old, worn-out furniture was adequate for group meetings. The only lighting came from a tall, gold-colored lamp with a flowery lamp shade. Charlie was elected spokesman. The CMC members were all ears when he explained the scenario at the hospital about the injection and consequent death of Max Weldon. "The first person to be contacted is Max Weldon's wife. Do you agree?"

"I've got her address right here," said Paul, "checking his cell."

"Dad said that the Weldons split up about six months ago. Maybe it's a crime of passion. Dad said she kept the house after the separation," said Trish.

"Mrs. Weldon is a prime suspect. Let's start with her. Trish, you should be the one to investigate her motive, but you need Charlie to drive; so Charlie, you should keep the car out of sight when you get there," said Josie.

"Another thing you want to do is to make sure she has been informed about the death before you spring into action. Otherwise, you might shock her," said Paul.

"You're absolutely right, Paul. Next Trish needs to snoop around the bank, questioning anyone who may be suspicious. Someone has to go back to the hospital. Trish, you and I have to visit Dad anyway; so we can snoop there. I'll text everyone as we get information," said Charlie.

The club split up for the time being with all members equipped with their cell phones.

CHAPTER 2

Saturday afternoon, Darcy Weldon, a sandy, brown- haired, middle-aged woman was in her kitchen having a cup of tea with her girlfriend and neighbor of the past five years, Joy Jensen, a blonde-haired, attractive woman. Darcy shared everything with Joy including her separation agreement with Max. "I'm so frustrated and annoyed with Max. He harasses me with unnecessary calls, threats, name-calling and complaints about the amount of support he has to pay. I know I'm fortunate that he pays my alimony with a two-week paid vacation every year but I'm suffering tremendously with the abuse I'm taking every day. Do I have to move? I need his money. Sometimes I wish he were dead."

"I know he's been a royal pain in the butt. You know, I've been best friends with you for five years and I've seen how you've been dragged down by his gigantic ego. Can you get a restraining order to protect you? If you are exasperated with the whole situation, then I can recommend the name of someone who can assist you."

At that moment, the doorbell rang. Darcy went to the door and was greeted by an RCMP officer. "May I help you?" she asked.

"My name is Sgt. Coady Freeman and I've come to…sorry ma'am…I've come to inform you that your ex-husband, Max Weldon, is dead."

"Dead? What happened?" choked Darcy, thinking about what she had just said in the kitchen to Joy.

"May I come in?" said the sergeant.

"Yes, please have a seat." She ushered him into her tidy, tastefully-decorated living room.

"It's a homicide, Mrs. Weldon. Max was killed by an overdose of morphine. Do you know anyone who wanted him dead?"

"I may have had thoughts but it wasn't me. I wouldn't actually kill him. I needed his support payments. What am I going to do for money now? I don't work and I haven't any income of my own. I was dependent on Max financially."

"Where were you last night between seven and nine?"

"I'm pretty sure I was home. I was talking to a friend and watching television."

"You're pretty sure? You can't even remember what you were doing last night," said Freeman.

"Yes, I do. I was…at home, here, watching T.V."

"Please take my card and if you think of anything, anything at all, call me." Detective Freeman saw his way out.

Darcy was nervous and agitated when she returned to the kitchen to share the news with Joy. "Max… murdered…at the hospital…last evening and I'm a suspect?"

"Slow down, girl. You mean Max has been murdered? What's going to happen now? I mean financially? Are you still in Max's will?"

"I don't know. I'm numb right now. You'd better go. I think I need to be alone for a while."

"Call me if you need me. Remember I'm here for you," said Joy.

"Thanks. You are a good friend. I'll call you soon. Bye."

Darcy flaked out on the chesterfield with a Kleenex box in her hand and started to cry. Was she crying out of grief…loss… worry…or just an emotional vent?

She didn't know how long she had been crying when the doorbell rang again. Darcy stumbled to the door, opened it and saw a young girl standing there. "Hello,"

Trish said. "My name is Trish Camden. My father is Staff Sergeant RCMP Rob Camden and he has had a heart attack. He is in the hospital in the room next to where your ex-husband was found murdered last night. My brother and I were there minutes before it happened and I'd like to come in to talk to you about it. Actually my brother is studying sociology at UPEI and when I grow up I want to be a detective just like my dad. We play sleuthing games at home when Dad is with us. We're getting pretty good at it too. I'd really like to come in and talk to you about your late husband. Would that be ok?" Trish was babbling, a sign of nervousness but she was a determined, charming girl and she knew it.

"As I was saying, I want to be a detective when I grow up; so I'd like to start here today on my very first case. May I come in, please?"

Darcy was exhausted from her tears and thought she might feel better with this young girl. *Maybe she'd be able to pick me up,* she thought. "My name is Darcy. Come in if you like. You say your dad had a heart attack? I know who your father is but I don't think he knows me."

Trish sat in a big armchair. "Dad will be ok but he'll need some extra rest when he gets home. Why I have come is to ask you a couple of questions about your relationship with your ex. Did he ever harass you?"

How does she know this? thought Darcy. "Yes. How do you know this?"

"Has Max been involved with another woman?" asked Trish bluntly.

"Look, I don't know who you think you are, kid, asking personal questions about my dead husband and his affair with whomever!"

"I'm sorry," Trish persisted, "do you know this other woman?"

"He has had several women. Erica Peabody was his secretary at the bank. Now please leave me alone." Darcy got up and showed Trish to the door.

"Do you know why someone would want him dead?" Trish continued.

"Lots of people." Darcy said. "Max had financial control over many people in Charlottetown, including me."

"Where were you last night between seven and nine p.m.?"

"I was here. I did not kill my ex-husband. Good- bye." Darcy slammed the door behind Trish.

Trish ran out of the yard, down the street, and around the corner where Charlie was parked. "How'd it go?"

"She's pretty upset. She said there was a love affair with Erica Peabody, Max's secretary at the bank. I think that's where we should head."

"I agree," said Charlie as he started the engine. The fifteen-minute drive to the bank had both of them chatting about this next visit. Charlie parked on University Avenue. The two of them made the short walk around the corner to the bank on Grafton Street. "Hopefully Erica Peabody works on Saturday," whispered Trish. "The bank will be closed soon." They entered the bank.

Charlie and Trish noticed the bank manager's office and then saw a very attractive, slim, long-haired blonde, thirty-five-or-so woman at a desk in the open area of the bank near Max Weldon's office. "Excuse me. Are you Erica Peabody?" asked Charlie. Then Trish directed Charlie's eyes to the name on the desk. "Oh, excuse me again. You must be Erica Peabody."

"Yes I am. How may I help you?" she answered. "I'm Charlie. This is my sister, Trish. We'd like to ask you a few questions."

"What kind of questions? Are you opening an account?"

"Well, no. We wanted to ask you about Max Weldon.

Has anyone spoken to you today about him?" "What business is that of yours?" snapped Erica.

"Our father is an RCMP officer and he is in the hospital in the room right next door to where Max was murdered. He asked us to come here to speak with you," Trish lied.

"The detective was here not more than an hour ago. I've told him everything I know." Erica said in a cool, distant tone.

Ms. Peabody looked at her watch. The bank closed in fifteen minutes. "I'm not going to discuss my private affairs with a couple of kids. Excuse me, but it's time for you to leave."

"Where were you last night between seven and nine p.m.?" Trish persevered.

"Good-bye." Erica got out of her chair, escorted them to the front door, and locked it behind them.

Charlie and Trish needed time to process these two interviews and were hungry; so they went back to their home in Cornwall where Nana was preparing supper and to get a fresh outlook on the situation. *So Freeman was ahead of them,* thought Charlie. Charlie sent a text to the club to give them an update. Immediately John sent a text back saying that Darcy was not at home between seven and nine last night as she had told the Camdens. Josie saw her on Facebook on University Ave. near Papa Joe's. Trish was in the kitchen with Nana cooking supper, spaghetti and veggies. She heard Charlie mention Josie's text but didn't respond. Then Charlie began texting.

"Hey, Trish, Erica Peabody was not home last night after seven p.m. either. I've got pictures of her on Facebook at Hunter's with some guy." Charlie and Trish wondered if Darcy and Erica told the same story to Freeman. "How did you come up with those pictures?" asked Trish as she placed the spaghetti on the table.

"Let's say I've got connections."

"So they've both lied to cover up their locations last night. Why?"

"That's a question we should ask Dad when we see him tonight. I bet Freeman doesn't have access to this info."

Charlie received another text, this time from John. "I've checked into the RCMP through my dad. He has access to phone calls made between Erica Peabody and Max Weldon. Although he isn't permitted to share this confidential information, I got a great peek at some papers he left on his desk at suppertime."

"This is an amazing mystery club," said Charlie. "John's on top of Erica's and Max's telephone calls."

"Great stuff," said Trish. "We'd better get ready to go see Dad."

The hospital was calm. The police team had left, but the yellow strips cordoning off room 227 remained. Rob was feeling tired, as the day had been rather unsettling with all the commotion. Charlie and Trish didn't want to drain their dad with too many questions; so they sat quietly beside his bed. "Hi, kids. Have you solved any mysteries today?"

"Not yet," Charlie said, "but we are following a new train of thought."

"When will you be released, Dad?" asked Trish. "Tomorrow's Sunday. The doctor said he'd see me in the morning and if all goes well, he may discharge me tomorrow. How's your school work, Trish? And how are your UPEI courses coming along, Charlie?"

"Fine," they said simultaneously. They wanted to share Charlie's murder investigation news. "Dad," said Trish, "can you tell us anything, even the least bit significant, about Max Weldon and his wife, Darcy?"

"Well, let me see. Max was in my room the morning of his surgery and death. He was talking about the fact that Darcy and he were unable to have any children and how disappointed they were about that. He also mentioned they had separated six months ago."

"Trish interviewed Darcy today after Sgt. Freeman had been there. She was still in shock about Max's death and she said she had been home when the murder took place but she wasn't, as I found pictures of her on Facebook hanging out on University Ave. near Papa Joes," said Charlie.

"Charlie also found pictures of Erica Peabody, Max's secretary, whom he was having an affair with, on Facebook at Hunter's during the time of the murder. Detective Freeman had also been to see her at Scotiabank before we arrived to question her," said Trish.

"I should have known you'd be into this case, especially when I can't be home to help you. Listen, they may have reasonable reasons for not telling the truth. Go home and get some sleep. Nothing will be happening on Sunday and you have school and courses next week; so you really don't have time to get involved in this situation."

The sleuths looked at each other and silently agreed to head out for the night. Their father was not able to continue this kind of conversation. He was going to need plenty of rest, not only physical rest, but emotional and mental rest as well.

CHAPTER 3

Darcy Weldon's filing system was meticulous. She knew where every income tax form, every bank statement, even her car service statements, were kept. Today she was looking at the will that she and Max had written together in the early years of their marriage. She sighed in remembrance of this useless piece of legality. Max wasn't as organized and orderly about things. Was there a remote chance he hadn't changed the old will upon separation? *Hardly*, she thought. Yet it began to needle her that it might be a possibility. She hadn't bothered to look at it. After all, he was the one with the savings account, not her. The old will stated that Max was to leave Darcy all funds in all accounts, RRSPs, the house, and cars. Darcy looked at the legal firm letterhead. It was half past ten on Monday morning. She called the lawyer who had signed the document. "Hello Ron. It's Darcy Weldon speaking."

"Oh Darcy, I'm so sorry about Max's death. I read about it in the Guardian this morning. I suppose you are wondering about the will?"

"Oh, that old thing has been around for years," said Darcy.

"Yes it has, but I've checked into it this morning and there have been some changes to the existing will."

"Really?" *Oh no,* she thought.

"I'm sure of it. After the memorial service I'd like us to sit down and go through it. I'll round up his bank statements in the meantime. When is the memorial service?"

Darcy was flabbergasted. "The service is tomorrow at 2 p.m."

"I'll be there. Good-bye."

Trish and Charlie picked up their dad at the hospital on Sunday afternoon. He was glad to be home. Trish and Nancy made one of Dad's favorite meals, adobo with rice and a salad. Nana was happy to see Rob at home and made a big fuss about staying quiet and peaceful. The kids spent the evening sharing news about the murder investigation. Charlie and Trish felt free to put time into the crime since they could stagger study breaks from school and university. Too much time together wasn't a good thing, as they started to pick on each other; so Charlie took off on Monday morning to meet up with Freeman at the hospital.

"Good morning," said Charlie to Sgt. Freeman. "Did you find anything of interest on the examination of the orderly uniform and other items found at the crime scene?"

"Not on the uniform but I found a long, blonde hair in the brown wig and I will send it off to Halifax to have a DNA test done on it."

"How long does it take for a DNA result to come back from Halifax?"

"It takes three weeks to a month if all goes well," said Freeman.

Charlie was disappointed to think it would take so long for this forensic procedure. His mind was a whirl. He knew exactly who had long, blonde hair.

"If I bring in a sample from someone I think may be involved in this case, would you be able to send it to Halifax for a DNA match?"

"Yes, I could," said Sgt. Freeman, but I must come with you. It's RCMP protocol."

Charlie and Freeman took off on a mission and they didn't have time to waste.

They departed from the hospital, and drove out of the parking lot and headed downtown to Scotiabank. *Charlie didn't need to see Erica Peabody. He needed a sample of her DNA. That's all. How was he going to get it? He had to be very careful and not do anything illegal.*

It was 10:30 a.m. when they entered the bank. Erica Peabody was not at her desk. *Could she be on her coffee break?* No. Her mug was in plain sight. *Oh no, I mustn't steal that,* he thought. *Oh, there she is in the back corner of the bank talking to a teller.* Her back was turned. Charlie pointed at the waste paper basket. There was a wad of gum lying on top of a piece of paper. Charlie nodded to Freeman who nodded back to Charlie. This was the signal for Charlie to pick up the paper before anyone would notice. In a flash he dropped it into a plastic bag held out by Freeman. They darted out of the bank. Charlie sent a text to the club. Most of the club members' cell phones were on vibrate which meant they were in class.

Freeman took the gum sample and sent it priority post with the blonde hair to the Halifax forensics crime lab. The worst part of the whole investigative process was the waiting for results to come back from Halifax. Charlie shared the fact with Freeman that Erica also lied about her whereabouts on the night Max Weldon was killed. "Facebook pictures show Erica at Hunter's for a portion of that night," said Charlie

"This is all circumstantial evidence. We are both curious about Erica's involvement in this crime. Please remember the police procedures and be patient for the results from Nova Scotia."

Charlie was glad Trish wasn't with them. She hated waiting for anything. Charlie was excited about being on top of the case and Freeman was dubious, yet somewhat curious, about Charlie's train of thought.

Rob Camden wasn't a joyful patient. He wanted to get up and get moving. That is what he always did to combat stress. Sitting around, reading the newspaper five times a day, doing the crossword puzzle, playing cards with his mom, and not getting enough exercise made him an unhappy, restless person. He knew today was the day of the memorial for Max Weldon and he knew he wasn't able to leave the house. Charlie and Trish knew about the memorial as well but they had classes all day and the only way they could possibly attend was to skip school. It wasn't too difficult for Charlie to skip, as he wasn't noticed in the large classes at UPEI but for Trish, who desperately wanted to be there, it was almost impossible not to be noticed. A call would go home about her absence and Dad would be angry. "Blah, blah, blah," she'd hear his reprimands about missing school to follow a lead in the case. She couldn't do this to her father, but she couldn't stand her brother getting a head start on solving the case.

Rob didn't want to know the actions of his sleuth team. *Better to be blind to their plans concerning attendance at the memorial,* thought Rob. *I'd like to be there myself.*

He knew the crowd at a memorial might bring forth more suspects and seeing Darcy Weldon's reactions would be of interest.

Trish was resigned to Charlie's attending the memorial at 2 p.m. The CMC was informed but no one could miss school. Josie and John, Sgt. Freeman's twins, definitely wouldn't dare meet up with their father at the memorial. Paul, the hacker of the club, sent a text to Trish that the license plate number of the truck that had swerved and ran Charlie and Trish into the ditch belonged to someone by the name of Hadar Whitney. No one in the club had heard of him. Paul said he'd dig up more information on this character when he had time.

Charlie prepared himself for the memorial service by devoting time to the suspect list. It was 1:45 when he arrived at the church hall to pay respects to the family. Darcy was dressed in black, wearing a skirt and blouse with matching earrings and necklace. She had her brother beside her who made the effort to fly to Charlottetown and take a week's vacation from his teaching job in South Korea, and that was all she had for family. People started gathering in the church sanctuary. Charlie noticed an attractive woman in a navy suit with blonde hair, a middle-aged man in a gray suit and burgundy tie, a couple from the bank where Max had worked, Erica Peabody, and the RCMP representative, Sgt. Freeman. A few other stragglers came in at the last minute. Charlie glanced at the retired school teacher he recognized from his elementary school days, the barber, the grocery store clerk, another woman with long, blonde hair and at the last minute another blonde-headed woman sliding into the last row.

The service was brief with the eulogy given by the retired school teacher. The committal was at the graveside with a reception in the funeral home afterwards. The refreshments were catered by the funeral home and consisted of punch, some crackers and cheese, and a fruit tray. *Darcy was holding up quite well,* thought Charlie. He noticed the woman in the navy suit comforting Darcy. She had her arm around Darcy and led her to the reception hall.

Charlie surveyed the scene carefully but he wished Trish were here with her photographic memory. There were three women with long, blonde hair; the one in the navy suit holding on to Darcy, and the other two that arrived late. One was wearing a casual pants and blouse outfit while the other was dressed for a party, black dress and high-heel shoes. *If I am to get anywhere in this investigation and keep an eye on Freeman, I've got to make myself known at the reception,* thought Charlie.

Darcy was alone while her friend was helping herself to punch. Charlie took this opportunity to introduce himself. "Hello, Darcy, I'm sorry for your loss," said Charlie. "I'm Staff Sergeant Rob Camden's son, Charlie Camden." Just then the woman in the navy suit returned with two glasses of fruit punch. "Darcy felt obligated to introduce them. "Joy, this is Charlie Camden. Charlie, this is Joy Jensen." *Now* thought Charlie, *I have a name for one of the blondes here.* Charlie asked, "Have you lived in Charlottetown very long, Joy?" Charlie noticed Joy's lack of interest in making conversation, as all she said was, "Five years."

"How do you know, Max?" Darcy asked Charlie. "Everyone in Charlottetown has heard of Max as the bank manager at Scotiabank. That is where I have my bank account."

Darcy was satisfied with this answer. Joy excused herself so she could mingle with other guests but it wasn't too long before Freeman was talking with her. Charlie wished he could overhear their conversation.

Charlie noticed one of the other blonde women talking to Erica Peabody. Charlie got up his courage to sidle into the conversation. "Hello, Erica. I'm sorry for your loss."

"It's Charlie, isn't it? I'm wondering why you are here?" asked Erica.

"Just thought I'd pay my respects to the bank manager's family," said Charlie. "Are you going to introduce me to your friend?"

"Look Charlie, I've said it before. I have nothing to say to you or your nosey sister," said Erica in a huff.

"My name is Susan. Susan Ramsey," she interrupted. "I went to school with Max a long time ago. We haven't seen much of each other but I did see him on occasion at the bank."

Once Erica saw that Susan spoke to Charlie, she quickly walked away. Charlie continued to show interest in getting to know Susan, this middle-aged woman, by adding, "have you known Erica long?"

"Oh no, we just met. She's much younger than me. No, I came today as Max and I use to play together when we were young children. We'd play make-believe games together with a couple of other girls in the neighborhood."

"Where did you live back then?" asked Charlie. "We grew up on Westview Drive."

Charlie noticed that Darcy was talking to the man in the gray suit. He looked like a banker or lawyer.

Susan was easy to talk to. She appeared comfortable, relaxed and calm. "Where do you work, Susan?"

"Oh, I'm retired. How about yourself, Charlie, are you a student?"

"I attend UPEI but I've taken the afternoon off to attend this memorial service. Did you know there is evidence that Max's death was not of natural causes?"

"I've heard that, but I can't imagine why anyone would want to harm him. My memories of Max are fond and fun. We use to play hide-and-go-seek, tag, and card games. But that was a long time ago. Situations and relationships change; we grow up."

Charlie was getting a good impression of Susan. "If you'll excuse me, Susan, I must talk to a couple of other people."

"It was nice to meet you, Charlie. See you around."

Charlie headed to the punch bowl where Joy was getting a refill. "How is Darcy holding up?" he asked.

"She's a strong woman. She'll do fine," said Joy.

Charlie was itching to investigate her whereabouts on the night of the murder but didn't want an emotional scene. Instead he asked, "Do you live near Darcy?"

"I live across the street from her."

Charlie's curiosity got the best of him. "I'm sure Darcy confided in you about Max since their separation. Can you help me understand why anyone would want to wish him dead?"

"I don't know why. He was very mean to my friend, Darcy. Please excuse me."

Quickly she cut short her conversation with Charlie and went back to Darcy's side.

Charlie wished Trish's photographic memory were here. He tried to analyze the characters at the reception. He looked around. There was one more woman Charlie wanted to meet, the party-dress girl. She was talking to the retired school teacher when Charlie interrupted the conversation, "You gave a wonderful eulogy," he said to the retired school teacher. "I'm Charlie Camden and you are…?"

"I'm Mrs. Ethel Jones and this young lady is Gretchen Zimmerman," said Mrs. Jones.

"I'm pleased to meet you. What a beautiful dress," said Charlie. "Did you find it in Charlottetown?"

"Actually, I got it in Montreal last year on a shopping spree with a friend."

"How do you know Max Weldon?" asked Charlie. "Oh, Maxwell was such a dear. He'd buy me expensive gifts on the side, you know," Gretchen said in hushed tones. "He and I planned getaway weekends. Maxwell bought this dress for me on a rendezvous in Montreal."

"What kind of work do you do?" asked Charlie. "I'm a nurse at the hospital. I was on call the night Maxwell died," said Gretchen, shivering at the thought.

Charlie was intrigued by this woman's life. "Did you see anything suspicious that night?"

"Well, Ted Jones, an orderly, and I brought Maxwell out of the recovery room and wheeled him into the room in unit 2," said Gretchen as she flicked her beautiful blonde hair. "After that I resumed my nursing duties in unit 4. I didn't see anything more. I heard the code blue when I was heading for unit 4. It wasn't until the next day that I heard Maxwell was dead. It's so sad. No more excursions to Montreal. I'm wearing this dress to remind me of our fun times."

Charlie saw several people put their punch glasses down by the empty punch bowl. He noticed Sgt. Freeman, with rubber gloves, pick up several glasses and place them in sterilized plastic bags. "Hey, Sergeant, are you looking for DNA matches to the blonde hair in the brown wig?"

"You're absolutely right."

"Are you going to send these off to Halifax?" asked Charlie.

"That's my plan."

The main suspects had left and the funeral director started to help the servers clear the tables. Freeman quickly left the funeral home, took his car and drove out of the parking lot and went home to prepare the package for the courier.

"Can you please send this package to Halifax?" asked Detective Freeman as he arrived at the courier office shortly before closing time.

"It won't go out today. I'll send it off in the morning." "Thanks," said Sgt. Freeman.

Back at the reception Charlie helped with the cleanup. When everything was in order, he left and headed for home. He texted the Camden Mystery Club once he drove into the driveway. He knew Trish and Dad would like to hear all the news.

CHAPTER 4

Precisely three weeks later Sgt. Freeman received the results from the Halifax crime lab. The report stated, "our forensics team checked and rechecked the DNA on this gum sample. It doesn't match the DNA of the blonde hair in the brown wig. We have checked the syringe and detected traces of morphine."

Charlie was pleased with the results on the syringe but deflated about the gum DNA not matching up with the blonde hair from the wig. *Back to the club,* he thought. He didn't want to apologize to Freeman; so all he said was "see you around."

Sgt. Freeman said, "the case isn't over yet, Charlie. We still have to get the results from the punch glasses. See you."

Charlie sent a text to the club with his disappointing news.

Rob Camden was glad to be home. Strict orders from the doctor were to rest in bed, take slow walks on the main floor of the house, and not to go up and down stairs. Nancy was a blessing. She prepared light lunches and kept him entertained by playing crib, forty-fives, and crazy eights. His nitroglycerin was for emergency use only; i.e., to put drops under his tongue whenever he had chest pains.

Trish was disappointed with Charlie's clue about Erica Peabody. When she got home from school, she discussed it with Dad who was resting on the couch with a book in his hand. "Hi, Dad, how was your day?"

"It was fine. I read, watched a bit of TV, and your grandmother plays a mean game of crib. She beat me three times. How was school?"

"Exams are coming up in a couple of weeks and I've got a lot of studying to do. Have you heard from Charlie today?"

"No. Why?"

"We were investigating Max's love affair with Erica Peabody. Sgt. Freeman received a report today showing the results from the forensics team in Halifax on the blonde hair and the gum from Erica Peabody's waste paper basket. The DNA from the blonde hair in the brown wig didn't match the DNA on the gum," said Trish.

"I'm lost. What blonde hair?"

"Well, a few weeks ago when Charlie went to meet Sgt. Freeman at the hospital. Freeman said he found a blonde hair in the brown wig we found in the trash can in unit 2, supposedly belonging to whoever wore the wig."

"Oh, I see. So Charlie saw that Erica had blonde hair and put two and two together and he and Sgt. Freeman found the gum sample in her waste paper basket. Well, he eliminated one of your prime suspects. Have you got any more suspects besides Darcy Weldon?"

"Not right now." Just then Charlie arrived home; so he sat down in the living room with Dad while Trish got up to help Nana in the kitchen.

Charlie kept his cell phone within reach and after supper several messages from the mystery club came in to console him and to make suggestions as to where to go from there. He knew the club couldn't meet at the clubhouse in the basement so soon after Dad's return from the hospital. *Suspects. What they were dealing with was a lack of suspects. He mulled the whole scene over and over in his mind. Trish's photographic memory must be able to trace something.* After the cleanup in the kitchen, Charlie approached Trish to rehash some of the scenes from the night of the murder. They left their dad alone in the living room while they headed down to the clubhouse.

"Think, Trish. We've got to look at the evidence we found in the washroom in the hospital and try and retrace our steps from the night of the murder when we were saying good night to Dad. Do you remember the person who wheeled the patient, Max, into the room beside Dad?"

"Yes, vaguely. A nurse and an orderly were the ones to wheel him into room 227 next to Dad's."

"That's right."

"Hold on a minute, Charlie."

"I remember that the orderly had his head down so we couldn't get a good look at him," said Trish. "Do you remember?"

"Not really. I remember we said good night to Dad and just after that we saw Max's body being wheeled into the room next door."

"You don't remember the orderly?" "No."

"Why would he have his head down as if he didn't want to be recognized?" asked Trish. "Then we heard the code blue alarm for unit 2 and so we headed over to check on Dad and see if he was ok. There were people gathered around room 227 at that time but we were so worried about Dad, relieved that he was ok that we didn't pursue any other information that night and headed for home. That's when we got driven off the road. Paul said the license plate number belonged to a Hadar Whitney. Do you think he has anything to do with our case?"

"Probably not but we can check it out," said Charlie.

"It wasn't until Saturday morning that we found the evidence in the washroom. That was just a hunch on my part."

"That stuff we found in the washroom was stashed there after the murderer gave Max the injection of morphine Friday night," said Charlie. "Then he slipped away when the code blue sounded as the nurses and doctors surrounded Max's room."

Trish was deep in thought. Suddenly she bolted upright. "The orderly with the nurse, the one wheeling the bed into room 227 didn't wear a wig."

"How do you know that?"

"His head was down but he didn't have a hat on and I distinctly remember seeing black hair, real hair. So there must have been another orderly, our fake orderly, who wore a brown wig."

CHAPTER 5

Charlie and Trish were constantly being interrupted by Camden Mystery Club test messages. The club Was gung-ho to hear about the memorial event and the glasses being collected for DNA. Things settled down by 10:00 p.m. which gave the siblings time to study. Lights were out at eleven for Tris, and Charlie began reading his sociology book for tomorrow's class. By 2:00 a.m. the two were dreaming, surmising, and imagining the eventual outcome of the DNA match.

The waiting period passed and the forensics team in Halifax examined the glasses from the memorial service. Trish was busy with her school projects and Charlie with his sociology courses. Paul and the twins were also heavily involved with homework. The day of the DNA results arrived and Freeman shared his news with the Camden household. He said he'd wait until they met up with him at RCMP headquarters to review the facts.

Charlie woke at 7:00 a.m., showered, dressed, ate his breakfast and tore out of the yard in the family car. He sprinted in the door of the RCMP station meeting up with Sgt. Freeman. The results which had come in late yesterday were being reviewed by

Corporal Frank Brown. "You're looking for conclusive evidence that someone drank out of one of those glasses and that someone has the same DNA as the blonde hair in the wig. There was no match."

"That can't be. I am sure I picked up the correct glasses at the memorial service last month. Charlie, did you see me?"

"I'm sorry, Sgt. Freeman. I'm as disappointed as you are. I thought I saw you pick up the right glasses but I'm not sure. If Trish had been with us, we'd have a definite answer but you must have missed the right glass."

"Darn it!" shouted Freeman.

"I have to head off to classes now," said Charlie. "I'll be seeing you."

Freeman shuffled into his office in a glum mood.

Charlie sent a text to Trish and the club members about the disappointment of the day and decided to call a meeting for 5:00 p.m. at their home. The twins arrived on time with Paul being fifteen minutes late arriving with a pizza.

"I'd like to open the meeting with the news I received this morning. Either Sgt. Freeman made a major blunder or we have the wrong suspects. The DNA was not a match on any of the punch glasses collected by Sgt. Freeman. Gretchen Zimmerman, Joy Jensen, Erica Peabody, and Susan Ramsey were the blondes I remember from the funeral reception. Sgt. Freeman did not pick up glasses that match the blonde hair in the brown wig," said Charlie. "Does anyone know what direction we take from here?"

Josie and John whispered to each other in the corner. "Should we say something or keep our mouths shut?" asked John. John nodded to Josie to speak.

"This news is personal, yet it may have an impact on the case. Which is more important?" whispered Josie. The Freeman twins stood up.

"Ah, we may have a little information that might shed some light on Dad's behavior at Max Weldon's memorial. He has been having some bouts of forgetfulness and the night before the memorial Mom and Dad had an argument. What I'm trying to say is it could have been easy for him to make a mistake," said Josie.

Trish and Charlie were surprised at the twin's open response about their dad. Charlie spoke, "I kept an eye on your dad but I wasn't fully aware of his whereabouts. Oh, Trish, I wish you could have been there."

"Well, where do we go from here?" asked Trish. "I think we should research some of Gretchen Zimmerman's history. After all, she was right at the crime scene. She may have lied about her whereabouts at the memorial."

Charlie asked, "Who would like to look into this with me?"

"I will," said Josie.

"Great," said Charlie with a smile.

"Susan Ramsey seems to be legit but we should check out her story," said Trish.

"I'll look into her story," said John.

"Joy Jensen's story should be verified," said Charlie. "Trish, I think you should check her out. You have already met Darcy, and Darcy and Joy are good friends."

"I think we should reinvestigate the truck that drove you guys off the road," said Paul. "It was the night Max Weldon was murdered and I checked the license plate which belongs to a person by the name of Hadar Whitney. I also did a little research on the fellow and found out he's on parole for drug trafficking and spent three years in prison. He just got out six months ago. I have an address in a trailer park on the outskirts of Cornwall. Maybe he will be a source of information for us."

"You certainly did your homework, Paul. Ok, I think we should look into this character. It wouldn't hurt," said Trish. The CMC decided to go forward with these options. Josie and John reminded the club that what was said in the room stays in the room and trusted the group to keep this policy. It was agreed. The club adjourned with the hope that all would have success with their assigned suspects.

After school Charlie and Josie decided to head back to the QEH to see if Gretchen Zimmerman was on call and find out if she was telling the truth about being on Unit 4 the night of the murder. They went directly to Unit 4 and asked at the nurse's station for Miss Zimmerman. Luckily she was on duty, so they waited for an opportunity to speak with her. She came out of a patient's room and was coming to the front desk when she saw them. She was surprised.

"What are you doing here?"

"Do you remember meeting me at the memorial service for Max Weldon?" Charlie asked.

"Yes, but I'm working right now. I don't have time to talk."

"This is my friend, Josie. We are sorry to arrive here unannounced but we have a few questions for you. Could we meet on your break or come by your home?"

"I have a fifteen- minute break in half an hour. I will meet you in the cafeteria."

"We will wait there for you. Thank you," said Charlie.

Gretchen was startled by two teenagers coming to her place of work. She wondered what kind of questions they had for her. She knew she had been rather open about her affair with Max, wearing her black party dress to the funeral and speaking so offhandedly about trips to Montreal. What she didn't tell

Charlie at the reception was how long the affair had been going on and how much she wanted Max to get a divorce.

Gretchen was good at putting on an extroverted, friendly mask. These kids weren't the cops and she had already spoken to them. *I don't owe them anything. She was allowing herself to get agitated about bothering to waste her break on two teenagers.*

Charlie bought Josie a hot chocolate while they waited for Gretchen. Josie had a crush on Charlie although he didn't know it. She had known him all her life and he always treated her with kindness but never thought of her as a girlfriend. He was so much older than her. He was eighteen and Josie was turning fifteen in a couple of weeks.

Gretchen kept her word but became irritated at their appearance at the hospital. "So you have some questions for me? I don't have much time and I have told everything to the police."

"We are part of a mystery club and Max Weldon's death has us questioning some of his contacts. If you don't mind, I'd like to know how long had you and Max known each other and how did you meet?" asked Charlie.

"We met at a party probably ten years ago. He was charming and funny." Gretchen's mood lightened as she spoke of him. "Max and I saw each other privately for the last five years, as his marriage was deteriorating and he needed some fun in his life. I gave him an escape from reality and he gave me wonderful shopping trips to Montreal. I miss him, but I didn't kill him. I was on duty the night he died. Ted Jones, an orderly, and I had brought Max down to Unit 2 from recovery and then I went directly back to Unit 4 on that night. You can check out my alibi with the head nurse on Unit 4. That is all. I must be getting back to my shift." Gretchen rose and paused to say, "Good luck with your search. Don't come to the hospital to see me again." And she was gone.

Paul found Susan Ramsey's mother's address on Westview Drive. He sent it to John Freeman by text. Trish met with John after school to visit Susan. Charlie drove them. "I'm going to Tim's for a coffee. I'll be back to pick you up," he said.

Trish rang the doorbell. Susan answered the door. "Hello, are you selling something?" she asked.

"Oh, no, my name is Trish Camden and my friend here is John Freeman. We are looking for Susan Ramsey. Would that be you?"

"Yes, I am. What can I do for you?"

"You met my brother, Charlie, at the funeral for Max Weldon and we have come to ask you a couple of questions about him."

"Are you members of some mystery club?" "Yes, we both are as well as a few others."

"My mother is quite old and she is in the living room. Come in and meet her and we can have a chat."

They stepped inside, took off their sneakers and allowed Susan to introduce them to her mother who was very hard of hearing. "Mom, these children are here for a visit. This is Trish Camden and John Freeman," she said pointing to the students and then she said to Trish and John, "this is my mother, Veronica." With the introductions made and the teenagers taking a seat in the small, overcrowded living room, Susan started to talk. "I moved back home a few years ago to take care of my mother. When I saw Maxwell's obituary in the paper, I decided to go to his funeral. Max and I were great buddies in the neighborhood as children."

Trish's sixth sense told her that Susan was truthful and very likeable. Nevertheless, her detective mind had to ask investigating questions. "Susan, what kind of work do you do?"

"I was a nurse in Kitchener, Ontario for twenty years but when my dad died and knowing how frail Mom was I came back to Charlottetown to look after her."

"Did you know what killed Max?" asked Trish. "No."

"He was given an overdose of morphine," said Trish, "how does one come by getting that drug?"

"I'm sure someone at a hospital would have access to that medication. I had Mom at the hospital for cataract surgery the week when Max was killed. I didn't even know he was in the hospital. How did you find out about his death?"

"My dad had a heart attack and was in the room next door to Max's room. Charlie and I were visiting our dad when the code blue sounded. It was pretty scary."

"I only found out about the death from the obituary. I know you must ask questions as part of your mystery club but I don't have any news to enlighten you with. As I said, Max and I grew up here on this street. I hadn't seen him since I moved back home." Susan looked over at her mom who was dozing in her chair. "Mom doesn't understand much of what we are saying. She has dementia. It's time I put her down for her nap. I have to go. Sorry I can't be of more help." Susan stood up and walked the teenagers to the door. "Thank you for seeing us," said Trish. "Yeah, thanks," said John.

Charlie was sitting in the old Toyota parked in the driveway, sipping his coffee and waiting for his sister and John. "How'd it go?"

"Fine. Susan lived in Kitchener and was a nurse for twenty years before she came back to PEI to live with her elderly mother. I didn't get the feeling that she had anything to do with the murder. She took her mom to the QEH the week Max was killed."

"For cataract surgery," added John.

"She says she only heard about the death from the obituary in the newspaper. I think she is telling the truth although who knows, she was a nurse and would be able to get around a hospital. It's just a gut feeling that she's telling the truth."

"If that's the feeling you get, then I think you should trust it, Trish. You still have to see Joy Jensen, Darcy Weldon's friend. When are you planning to visit with her?" asked Charlie.

"I'll check on Darcy tomorrow and ask her when would be a good time for me to visit with her friend, Joy."

"I'd like it if you and I checked out Hadar Whitney's trailer, Trish."

"Let's go there on the PD day on Friday."

"That's fine with me. I have no classes on Fridays."

Trish woke up in a cold sweat. She had been dreaming. Blond-headed people… many…swirling around her…flashbacks of the curly brown wig, the hospital, the intern coming towards her with a needle, trying to inject her, she started to run and was chased down a long hallway. She had no exit. The intern was just about to stick her with the needle when…Trish's heart rate was racing. She got up and had a glass of water. Went to the bathroom and then went back to bed. What did this dream mean? She pondered it for several minutes. The clock radio showed the time, 3:14 a.m. Trish's mind was working overtime.

She lay down trying to quiet her mind. She dozed off and awoke at 7.

Snow fell during the night. Trish met her nana in the kitchen. Nana had eggs and bacon out of the fridge but Trish wasn't hungry. "I'm going to have a piece of toast and a cup of tea," she said.

"Are you ok, my dear?" Nana asked.

"I'm fine; just had a bad dream last night. Is Charlie up yet?"

"I haven't heard him. I think he has classes today, but not until ten o'clock. Are you sure you don't want more for breakfast?"

"I'll be fine, Nana. I need a ride into town by 9:00

a.m. I'll ask Charlie when he gets up."

Trish sat with her tea and toast pondering the night's dream. Nana sat across from her with a bowl of porridge and a cup of tea. Neither spoke. When the clock on the stove said 8:15 a.m., Trish heard her dad and Charlie moving around, Charlie coming upstairs from the basement and Dad from the end of the hallway. Everyone congregated in the kitchen. Trish was getting antsy about getting to Darcy Weldon's, so she could make a connection with Joy Jensen. Charlie had told her about meeting Joy at the memorial service but Trish had never met her. "Hurry up, Charlie. I need a drive and you have to get to the university."

"Don't you have school today, Trish?" asked her dad. "It's a PD Day, Dad. Tomorrow is one as well." "I'm not going to ask you where you are going but I do want to know how you are getting home," said Dad.

"Paul has recently gotten his Driver's License. He will drive me home. Don't worry, Dad. Paul has taken driving lessons for six months. He's a good driver."

Charlie and Trish left Cornwall and headed for Darcy's home. "I told you that Joy lives across the street from Darcy. All you have to see Darcy for is to find out which house is Joy's and if Joy is at home."

"I know. I've got this, Charlie. Thanks for the ride." "See you."

Trish rang the doorbell. Darcy answered it. "Oh, it's you again. What do you want this time? More questions?"

"Just one, Mrs.Weldon. Could you please tell me which house belongs to Joy Jensen?" asked Trish.

"Whatever for? Are you going to interrogate her as well? She lives in the grey house over there." She pointed with her hand. "She's my best friend and I don't want you to be so nosey with her."

"I promise I won't. Sorry I've upset you. Have a nice day."

Trish bounded through the lightly-fallen snow towards Joy's house. She noticed Joy had a royal blue car in the driveway. She used her photographic memory to study the license plate. She sent a text to Paul to meet her at the address in about fifteen minutes. Boldly she rang the doorbell and waited for a response. There was none. She rang it again and then a third time before she heard someone coming to the door. The woman opening the door had long blonde hair and was wearing a bathrobe and slippers. "Yes?"

"Hello. My name is Trish Camden and I would like to ask you a couple of questions about the death of Max Weldon. Did you know him?"

"Cripes! I just got out of the shower. Darcy Weldon is one of my dearest friends and I've never met her ex but heard a lot about him. Look here. I'm not dressed for company and I have nothing to add to your inquisition." Trish was getting that sixth sense about Joy. Her annoyance and fact that she didn't know Max seemed too implausible. Trish was prepared for another door slam and she got it without another word.

Trish had a hunch Joy knew more, much more, and she wasn't saying a word. Trish left the house, kicked some snow with her sneakers, and walked around the neighborhood. What Trish didn't know was that Joy was on the telephone with her friend Darcy. "I know she's nosey. She's just a kid," said Darcy.

"What do you think about her tracking me?" asked Joy.

"I don't know why she arrived at your door. It's a good thing you didn't let her in. Why don't you come over for tea? I just made a fresh pot."

"I have a real estate house showing this morning. I'll take a rain check," said Joy,

"I noticed that girl just got picked up. Good riddance. I'll talk with you later, Darcy."

Paul questioned Trish about her investigation. She said it didn't go very well and she had a premonition that Joy was hiding something. She gave Paul the license plate number and when he got Trish to her yard he did a check on it. "That car is from Young's Auto Dealer."

"That doesn't make any sense. Why would Joy rent a car when she's lived here for over five years? Why wouldn't she just buy one or lease one? Thanks for the ride, Paul. Charlie and I are going to check out that other license plate you mentioned tomorrow."

With school being cancelled and Charlie not having classes, he and Trish took the opportunity to check Hadar's home. At 8:30 a.m. they turned into the trailer park looking for site 8. It couldn't be missed. Charlie and Trish saw a shabby, run-down, gray trailer with a broken window in the door, a scrawny dog sitting on the crooked steps and some kind of dilapidated, beat-up, rickety truck with the license plate RT 453. "This is the place," whispered Trish. The dog growled but Trish ignored him as they knocked at the door. No answer. They knocked again louder. They heard the sound of someone falling out of bed. Then the door opened and a skinny man snarled, "what the hell do you want? Cripes, it's only 8:30 in the morning."

Charlie spoke, "we're sorry, sir, for disturbing you but we have a couple of questions we'd like to ask you about your truck being in an accident. You see, my sister, Trish and I were run off the road and your license plate matched the truck involved in the accident."

"My truck? I doubt it. I don't know anything about that," said Hadar.

"You are Hadar Whitney, aren't you?" "What of it?"

"Well, we checked the records of the license plate and it belongs to Hadar Whitney. May we come in and ask you a couple of questions?" Charlie persisted.

"Do you have a search warrant?" "No."

"Get lost!" he said as he slammed the door.

"Wow, he's hostile even if it's because we arrived so early. Charlie, park the car out of sight and we'll wait for an opportunity to check out the trailer," said Trish.

"We have heard over and over from Dad that you need to get a search warrant before you enter someone's residence, Trish. Isn't that one of the first rules Dad has taught us?"

"Why don't we stake out the trailer this time, Charlie?" pleaded Trish.

"We'll have to cover the day with other club members then."

Charlie sent an immediate text to the club to obtain substitute investigators for latter parts of the day. Instantly Charlie heard back to stay put until Josie and John could cover the trailer and Hadar's whereabouts from 10:00 a.m. to 5:00 p.m. Paul offered to take the shift from 5:00 p.m. until 10:00 p.m. The day was covered. Trish and Charlie asked the club to keep them posted as to Hadar's comings and goings. Charlie and Trish surveyed the trailer park as they drove in and parked a good distance away from Hadar's site. They spied a dilapidated, weathered, old shack at the entrance to the trailer park; so they made their way over to it and luckily found it abandoned. The door was ajar. Trish pushed it open and found a single room with a beaten up, rotten wood floor and a dirty window which was in perfect position to view Hadar's trailer. Also they found a torn, worn sleeping bag bundled up in a corner. It was dry and comfortable, a great place for a stakeout.

Charlie had a pair of binoculars in the back seat of the car which he grabbed and placed around his neck. The siblings examined the shelter and decided to camp out in the shed watching for any movement from Hadar. The truck was still in the driveway; so they assumed he hadn't left the park. They didn't have to wait too long before they saw the scrawny-looking man that matched the description that Charlie had texted, leave the trailer and get into his broken-down truck. *Should they follow the truck or should they stay and check out the trailer?* Charlie and Trish decided they might get more evidence if they spied on the trailer. When Hadar's truck disappeared down the road towards Cornwall, the sleuths made their move. They walked up to the door of the trailer and knocked. They found the door wasn't locked and there was the scrawny-looking dog which barked and bared its teeth. This time Trish opened her backpack and brought out her lunch, a ham sandwich. Charlie said he'd go no further and disapproved of Trish's brazen self-confidence. *What to do now?*

Charlie stayed on the lookout while Trish entered the trailer, fed the snarly dog and tied him outside while she went inside.

The dingy, messy, smelly trailer was so full of clutter Trish didn't know where to begin. She followed her nose to a stash of marijuana and some huge plants. There in the open living room was the weed on a coffee table with an ashtray full of cigarette butts. But, on this table there was a pile of loose papers. Trish started to read and sort through the pile. It seemed to have some sort of order to it. She saw that some of the papers had a check mark on them and others did not. She started to place them into two categories. Then one of the pieces of checked papers leapt off the page at her as she read: brown-haired wig, orderly uniform, syringe filled with morphine, rubber surgical gloves, and a Charlottetown Hospital staff ID badge. "Hey, Charlie. Look at what I've found. Oh my gosh! Hadar had something to do with the murder of Max Weldon!"

An immediate response from Charlie outside the trailer said, "Don't sort the papers and GET OUT OF THERE QUICK!"

Why is he so angry? Get out of there quick. Doesn't sound like Charlie, but I'd better take his advice. What about the dog? Trish opened the door and pushed the dog in and slammed the trailer door behind it. They returned to the shack which was well-hidden by a clump of spruce trees and texted the club.

Trish was excited at the paper she saw in the trailer. "Charlie, Hadar is somehow connected to the murder. I know it. I feel it. The list is still in the trailer and we must get a search warrant in order to retrieve it before it is lost forever. We have to get Freeman to obtain a search warrant and get back here as soon as possible. It's almost as if Hadar was keeping a grocery list. All the items needed for the murder were written in a list one after the other down the page, just like getting ready to go to the supermarket but for the hospital instead."

"Calm down, Trish. We'll go to the police station and see if Detective Freeman is there."

"Do you think we should have taken the paper with us?"

Charlie was specific about getting out of there and leaving the papers.

"Definitely not. You could damage the evidence if you took it without a search warrant."

Charlie sent a text to Josie. They received a message from her that she and her brother were on their way to relieve them. They had to convince their mother to drive them there and explain the importance of this mystery club stakeout. Barb knew how important this club was to the twins and had many conversations about it with her husband and Rob. She felt their opinion took precedence over hers; so she prepared lunch for the twins and requested them to dress warmly although it was a mild, sunny day. She knew of the trailer park and Charlie had texted John that there was a shack to keep them comfortable. Just then Hadar's truck was spotted returning home. Charlie and Trish kept a watchful eye for any other movement until the twins arrived.

Josie and John arrived with their mother. "Now, you kids be careful. I'm not happy about this. You are too young to be doing undercover work. You're just like your father. If Rob Camden knew what was going on without his permission, he'd have another heart attack."

Charlie and Trish told Mrs. Freeman that this was a very insignificant stakeout and nothing bad would happen. Mrs. Freeman knew she had to give her kids a sense of freedom. She said she would be back at 5 p.m. to pick them up and told them to keep their cell phones on and to stay out of sight. They told their mom not to worry and that they would text her every hour. Charlie passed the binoculars to John.

Barb left in her car and Charlie and Trish disappeared in their dad's car heading for home.

Josie, John and Paul had all received the text from Charlie about the list. This 'hospital list' that Trish had found was a breakthrough in the case.

Charlie was worried about the twins being fourteen-years-old and staking out a possible murder with no means of transportation to get away. Josie and John were well-informed about police actions and he didn't want them to cross the line by doing anything stupid similar to what Trish had done. Trish had entered the trailer without an official police-signed search warrant.

Josie and John had grown up with Trish. Rob Camden and Coady Freemen were good friends. The kids would play mystery games and the families would have family get-togethers. After Rob's wife passed and his mother, Nancy, moved in, the families were very close, always looking out for one another.

The twins waited and waited for some action around Hadar's trailer. It was 4:30 p.m. when they noticed a grey car pull up in front of his shabby home. A woman got out and made her way around the grungy dog and entered the trailer. She wore a beige jacket, a pulled-up hood, jeans, stylish boots, and carried a purple purse. The purse was compact. The twins noted all of this but couldn't detect a description of her face. She didn't stay long. She came out of the trailer with a small package and drove off. Josie texted Charlie who was home and he asked if she got the license plate of the grey car. Josie said it was a PEI plate TF 643. Charlie was proud of her detective work and praised her for it. He said he would get Paul to check out the license plate.

John and Josie's shift was up. Their mom arrived to take the twins home, bringing Paul with her. It was five o'clock and Paul came loaded down with a bag full of munchies. Paul had already found the owner of the grey car. It belonged to Young's Auto Dealer. Trish and Charlie were surprised when they got the text from Paul.

"What do you think of that?" asked Trish.

"How the heck do we link Hadar Whitney to the crime? He doesn't have blonde hair. Well, we can't give up now," said Trish.

Trish and Charlie were home for supper with their dad and Nana. Meanwhile Paul munched and snuggled up in the ancient sleeping bag in the dilapidated shack at the entrance to the trailer park. They got no further texts from Paul.

"What do you think, Dad?" asked Charlie.

"I think you need some proof, some concrete evidence. All you've got now is a woman arriving at Hadar Whitney's trailer and a list of items needed for a murder that you should never have seen, Trish. You have a wig with a blonde hair and four women at the funeral that have blonde hair. You might want to find out who rented the car from Young's Auto Dealer. You haven't made any connection between the woman whom you don't have an identity for and Hadar."

"You're right, Dad. Charlie and I get so excited at times that we put the cart before the horse and have to slow our thoughts down. Let's play a detective game using the information we have right now," said Trish.

"Ok, Trish," said Charlie.

"The brown wig had a blonde hair in it, we have that DNA but there is no match between them," said Trish.

"Erica Peabody, Susan Ramsey, Gretchen Zimmerman, and Joy Jensen all have blonde hair," said Charlie.

"The punch glasses picked up by Sgt. Freeman didn't prove any DNA match to Joy Jensen, Gretchen Zimmerman, or Susan Ramsey. Erica's gum didn't give a match either," said Trish.

"But, Freeman may have been careless at the memorial service according to the twins and might not have picked up the right glasses."

"Then what we heard today about the list of hospital items found at Hadar's place made it look as if he were involved somehow in the whole scheme of the murder. He may be an accomplice to the murder," said Trish.

"Who was the woman driving the dealership car out to Hadar's trailer? Even if we didn't get a perfect identification of her, we certainly can call Young's Auto Dealer and find out who rented that car. And one more thing we haven't mentioned. If the woman and Hadar are involved, we still have no motive

CHAPTER 6

Staff Sergeant Camden decided to intervene. He called Sgt. Freeman at his home that evening and explained the background information so he could obtain a search warrant of Hadar Whitney's home. Once he got off the phone, he turned to his kids and said, "Sgt. Freeman will get a search warrant and take one of you with him to Whitney's trailer. Charlie, I think it's Trish's turn. I've resigned myself about keeping you out of harm's way. I will call the dealership in the morning. I think they will be more favorable to sharing the information with me in regard to the rental of the car. For now, I want you two to be careful, especially you, Trish."

"Thanks, Dad," said Trish. "I'll be careful."

Sgt. Freeman, flustered and agitated, managed to get a search warrant from a courthouse judge and on boss' orders picked up Trish at school the next day.

He was not his usual confident self and Trish was able to spot this right away with her inquisitiveness. She remembered the twin's conversation about their parents and Freeman's showing visible signs of stress.

"How are you today? Did you have any problems getting a search warrant?" asked Trish.

"Yah, it's always a hassle at the courthouse and I've been a heck of a lot better."

"Do you know the way to the trailer park?" asked Trish. "Of course," he said, "be prepared for some flak." It was then that Trish noticed Freeman's handcuffs and gun.

Trish knew the procedure and she had already met Hadar under different circumstances; so she felt prepared. What she didn't know was Freeman's inner turmoil and how it would affect the situation they were heading for at Hadar's trailer.

The RCMP car pulled up and parked across the driveway of the trailer to avoid Hadar's escape with the truck. Freeman signaled Trish to follow him. He hammered at the door. "RCMP. Open up. We've got a search warrant."

The windows in the trailer were very small and the rear door was blocked with heaps and piles of junk. Hadar was caught up in his own mess. Freeman wasn't going to wait for Hadar to make a getaway. He took out his revolver and shot the lock off the main door. With Trish behind him they entered the trailer. Freeman grabbed Hadar and shoved him up against a wall, handcuffed him, and removed him from the trailer. Trish thought all of this took only a matter of seconds. Freeman pushed Hadar into the backseat of the car and locked him in while he and Trish put on their rubber gloves and began their search of the trailer.

"Phew, it stinks of weed in here," said Trish. She headed for the coffee table and its piles of papers. Trish knew exactly what she was looking for and wanted to retrieve it. She did, stuck the list in her pocket and kept searching for more evidence. Freeman climbed over mounds of compost, dirty clothes, and pots of marijuana plants. He came to a room where he found medical supplies, needles, straps of rubber used to expose veins, and a whole tray of chemical compounds which included morphine.

All of a sudden Freeman began to sweat, and his heart pounded and started to race. He was having a panic attack. He had had them before but never on the job. He knew what he had to do to overcome them. He slumped onto the floor and called out to Trish to bring him a glass of warm water.

"Are you ok, Sgt. Freeman?" asked Trish as she passed him the water.

"Can't talk now," he managed to say.

"What can I do for you?" asked Trish.

"Wait." Freeman was taking slow, deep breaths. *Yoga breathing,* thought Trish.

Trish felt helpless and didn't know if Freeman would get any better. Meanwhile Hadar was locked in the backseat of the RCMP car. The scrawny dog was nowhere in sight. Trish sent a text to her dad and within fifteen minutes Corporal Frank Brown was at the trailer. By that time Freeman was starting to come around and he began to speak in normal, coherent sentences. "I'm ok, Frank. It must have been a case of indigestion. Probably something I ate last night. Trish, did you find anything to use as evidence?"

"Yes. I found a list of supplies needed to carry out the murder of Max Weldon."

She handed the paper to Corporal Frank Brown. "Good. I found this room full of medical supplies, chemical compounds including morphine, and white powder which could be cocaine. It looks as if Hadar's been dealing in drugs for some time. I'll have to call it in and get a drug squad out here. We'll take Hadar in for questioning. And Trish, please don't mention my indigestion to anyone."

"No problem."

Corporal Brown's primary assignment was to question suspects upon arrival at the RCMP station.

He was well aware of Hadar Whitney, as he was the one who sent Hadar to prison five years ago. "You've broken your parole again, Whitney. I may add. Sgt. Freeman has found quite a stash of drugs, morphine, possibly cocaine, and a large supply of marijuana plants, all in that trailer of yours. I thought you would have been sick of prison by now. But no, you're looking at drug trafficking and perhaps murder."

"I didn't kill anyone," blurted Hadar in defense. "What is this?" Corporal Brown held up the piece of paper with the list of items needed at the crime scene at the Queen Elizabeth Hospital.

"You can't prove my involvement in the murder. It's not even my handwriting. Give me a piece of paper and I'll prove it," said Hadar.

"Write your name on this." Corporal Brown produced a blank piece of paper.

Brown, the graphologist on staff, carefully compared the two papers and Hadar was right. The penmanship was very different. "Where were you on the night of Saturday, November 16th?"

"I was home in my trailer." "Were you alone?"

"Yes."

"I have taken a statement from Trish Camden who says differently. She said she and her brother were run off the road by a truck with your license plate on it at around 7:00 p.m. Explain this."

"I loaned my truck to a friend. She was driving it." "Was she the one who wrote this list?"

Hadar was cornered in his own lies. He had to fabricate something fast. "Perhaps, I think. Yah, maybe she was the one who wrote this list. She's the one who borrowed my truck."

"Does she have a name?" asked Brown.

"I don't remember. You see, I talk to a lot of people every day; I can't jolt my memory."

"I hope you realize you are being charged with drug trafficking and possibly murder. Ok, Sgt. Freeman, he's all yours." Freeman and Trish came into the interrogation room. Hadar, still wearing handcuffs, was ushered out of the room and down a long corridor to a holding cell where he was kept. Trish followed Freeman back to the office. Her mind was whirling. *She…she…she was driving the truck.* Why hadn't that occurred to her before? It was impossible to actually see the driver of the truck on the night she and Charlie were forced off the road and whoever it was didn't stop; she couldn't stop if she was coming from the hospital after committing a murder. It all made perfect sense. A woman was at the trailer buying drugs, was in a conspiracy with Hadar, who was an accomplice to murder by supplying the items on the list to a **woman**. She performed the actual murder and then dropped off the clothes, wig, and other items in the trash can across from room 227.

"We need to bring Joy Jensen in for questioning," said Trish. Just then she turned to look at Freeman. He appeared to be having difficulty breathing. He was grabbing his chest. He seemed to be disorientated, and had difficulty swallowing. Saliva drooled from his mouth, and his head was under great pressure. He said in a whisper, "call 911".

CHAPTER 7

Freeman's panic attacks were becoming more frequent and this last one was diagnosed as a mental breakdown. He was hospitalized with a psychiatrist assigned to his case. Rob Camden was recovering nicely at home but as soon as he heard of Sgt. Freeman's stress attack and hospitalization he knew he had to visit him. Camden knew Freeman could not focus on the murder investigation now and maybe not ever again; so he told his teens not to expect Freeman in any further investigation of the murder.

Charlie drove his father to the hospital while Nana and Trish stayed home. It gave Rob an uneasy sensation to return to the hospital so soon after his own recovery there. Now he was to visit Freeman in Unit 9, the psychiatric ward. Rob told Charlie to wait in the lounge at the front door while he went to speak with Sgt. Freeman.

"Hello, Coady. How are you?" asked Rob Camden. Freeman was heavily sedated and his movements were slow and methodical.

"I'm…ok. Life…is…in…slow…motion," said Freeman. "Have…you…seen…my…family?"

"They'll be here this evening. I talked with Barb and she told me that she and the twins will be by after supper."

"Why don't we take a little walk to the common room? I'll help you up and steady you with my arm."

"Ok," said Freeman. Rob helped him up as Freeman shuffled his feet out of the room.

He guided Coady to a comfortable armchair and helped him into the seat. Freeman was drugged and helpless. He wouldn't be able to continue with the investigation. Josie and John hadn't been in the hospital to see their father yet and they were going to be in for quite a shock.

Rob began some sense of a conversation about work and how it led to all kinds of physical and emotional illnesses. And being over forty, one's body starts to deteriorate.

"Yah…I…know…you…had…a…heart attack… didn't… you?" said Coady in a slurred speech. His mind was fuzzy and he imagined prickly wires sticking out of his head. "I'm…tired… now. Can…you…help…me… to…my…room, Rob?"

"Yes, Coady," said Rob. " Good-bye Coady. I'll see you soon."

Rob and Charlie remained silent as they left the hospital and returned home. Rob pondered his visit and reflected upon it on the way home.

Trish was deep in thought as she mindlessly helped Nana prepare supper, a tossed salad with a cooked, frozen pizza. She felt for the twins wondering how they would cope. Without Sgt. Freeman able to work the case and Dad out on sick leave, it looked pretty glum for solving the mystery. The Camden Mystery Club must meet. They needed to update their data anyway. At supper Trish suggested to Charlie that the group get together the following day after school in the clubhouse. Professionally they wouldn't bring up Freeman's condition; also they wanted the twins to know how supportive they were. Charlie agreed and sent a text to the club after supper. Rob didn't interfere. He knew better than that. He just made himself scarce when the group came over.

The afternoon meeting was as lively as usual with Beach Boys music coming from the old record player in the corner. Once everyone was there, the record stopped and they got down to serious business. Josie and John Freeman were there and so Charlie opened the meeting with special sympathy to the twins for their dad's health. Then he began the update in regard to the Max Weldon mystery. "As you know, Sgt. Freeman was a wonderful, helpful RCMP officer to allow Trish and me to tag along with him on many police encounters. Without his involvement we would have been unable to venture alone. I asked my dad if we could watch suspects through the two-way mirror in the interrogation room when Corporal Brown questions someone. He will allow this and had already allowed Trish and Sgt. Freeman this privilege. The RCMP must assign the case to a new officer and that person has to be briefed. My dad will know who this is later today; so I'll let you know."

"Now for an update on the file," said Trish. "Freeman had a search warrant for Hadar's trailer and I was involved in the search. He handcuffed Hadar and locked him in the back of the RCMP car while we looked at the contents of the trailer. I found the paper with the list and recovered it as evidence. Meanwhile Freeman collected samples of drugs and drug paraphernalia. Hadar was brought to the police station for questioning by Corporal Brown. I've been thinking of Hadar as an accomplice to the murder. In the statement by Hadar, he implied that a woman wrote the list of items on the sheet of paper. Brown checked Hadar's handwriting and compared it to the writing on the paper. Hadar didn't write the list. Hadar said it was written by a *she* but he didn't say who the woman was. I think it's Joy Jensen but we don't have a DNA match yet. Does anyone have any ideas?"

"Why do you think **she** is Joy Jensen?" asked Paul. "I know she has blonde hair, she was abrupt with you, she has rented two different cars from Young's Auto Dealer, but what else are you basing your suspicion on?"

"Don't you think what you just said is evidence enough to call her in for questioning?" asked Trish. "What I'd like to hear from the club is how we are going to gather information about Joy Jensen. Do we have to go back and see Darcy Weldon to build an empathetic relationship with her in order to set up a more incriminating situation with Joy Jensen? I'm open for a group discussion."

"Before we follow Trish's train of thought," said Charlie, "I'd like for us to report on the other suspects from the last meeting. Josie and I went to the hospital and checked out Unit 4 and Gretchen's alibi about arriving there the night of the murder. It would be impossible for her to wheel Max into the room, change into the articles of clothing, inject Max, change into her nursing uniform and be on Unit 4 for duty in time for her shift. Therefore Josie and I are eliminating Gretchen Zimmerman as a suspect."

"Likewise, I looked into Susan Ramsey's story and visited neighbors on Westview Drive who knew the kids in the area and remembered Max and Susan as good friends. I really don't have any suspicions about her,"

said John.

"Susan is a very nice lady. She lives with her elderly mother. John and I have no evidence or suspicions about her."

"Trish, if you want to go ahead with your Joy Jensen case, then, let's talk about it now," said Paul.

There were some muffled voices in the room. John stood up and said, "Revisit Darcy and question Joy Jensen. Maybe we can't bring Joy to the RCMP station but we sure can check both of them at their homes. I'd like to volunteer to go with you, Trish, to see Darcy Weldon and I'd like to suggest that Charlie and Josie visit Joy Jensen."

"What was in the package that woman picked up at Hadar's trailer? That woman might have been Joy Jensen. Maybe she is involved in the drug scene as well as being a murder suspect," said Paul. "Didn't your dad say the grey car that was at Hadar's trailer was rented by Joy Jensen from Young's Auto Dealer and she rented a blue car from the same place. Why?"

"And what role does the man in the grey suit have in the whole picture? He may not have blonde hair but he appears to be someone significant."

The CMC became energized with new hope and direction. Josie also agreed to follow up with a visit to Joy Jensen's place with Charlie. John and Trish agreed to visit Darcy Weldon. The plans were set. The meeting was adjourned.

Trish and John got Paul to drive them to meet at Darcy's home the next day after school. They arrived at 3:30 p.m. There was another car in the driveway; so the two waited around the corner until the visitor left. They had a good vantage point of the house; so they just made small talk, looking inconspicuous, as they were delayed. Finally a tall man in a grey suit came out of the house, entered his car, and drove away.

Once the car was out of sight, Trish and John walked up to the house and Trish rang the doorbell and were met by Darcy Weldon who looked shaken at the news she just heard. Trish introduced John to Darcy and asked if they could come in for a few moments. "It's you again. Trish, I see you've brought a friend, John, you say?"

"Yes. We belong to the same mystery club," said Trish. As bold and brazen as she always was, she asked,

"Who was that man that just left?" "He is my lawyer," said Darcy.

"You appear to be upset. Did he say anything to alarm you?"

"I don't wish to discuss the will with you kids," said Darcy.

"Oh, you mean Mr. Weldon's will. We understand.

It's none of our business."

"Why are you here?" asked Darcy.

"We've been feeling so very sorry for you; we just felt like paying a social call," said Trish. "Can I make you a cup of tea?"

Darcy's stomach was full of pain and her heart was heavy; so she thought a cup of tea sounded good. "Yes, I shall make tea for the three of us," she said. "Please come in."

While Darcy went to the kitchen, John and Trish surveyed the living room. Trish spied a folder from a legal firm in plain sight on the coffee table. The lawyer must have left it with Darcy. Trish flipped it open and saw the contents of Max Weldon's will. Quickly she read the basic contents. Darcy was executor of the estate. Darcy remained in the matrimonial home and inherited Max's TFSA, but Erica Peabody and Gretchen Zimmerman were to receive all stocks and bonds and his Registered Retirement Savings Plan. John knew what a TFSA, a Tax Free Savings Account was, as he was studying money and banking in school and it had just been on the last test he had. Trish closed the folder as Darcy walked in with a tray of cookies, a pot of tea, and china tea cups. She went through the motions of being a gentle host but her heart wasn't with them. She was wallowing in despair. *How could he leave all his money to those other women? What are TFSAs anyway? I have a house but no money. How can I get a job at my age? I've never worked and I have no skills,* thought Darcy. Trish seemed to read Darcy's mind when she asked, "Did you receive bad news from your lawyer?"

"I think it's bad news," said Darcy, "Max left the house to me; that's the good part; however, all his investments are being left to Erica Peabody and someone by the name of Gretchen Zimmerman, two women he was having affairs with. I have no money to support myself. I'm too young for the Old Age Security.

What am I going to do? My lawyer said something about my inheriting Max's TFSA, whatever that means. It doesn't sound like money to me. Do either of you know what it is?"

John spoke, "I just studied TFSAs for a test I wrote in my money and banking class. A TFSA is a special account you can use as a savings account which permits you to save money without paying tax on it. They are called Tax Free Savings Accounts. Go to the bank and find out how much it is worth."

"I don't want to do anything. I just want someone to take care of me," cried Darcy. "I must talk to my friend, Joy. She always has something to cheer me up."

Trish gave a you-know-who glance towards John and he rolled his eyes in response. "How long have you and Joy been friends?" asked Trish.

"She moved into the neighborhood about five years ago. I trust her completely with all my problems and childhood stories. She has been so understanding since Max and I separated."

"How is Joy employed?" asked Trish.

"Oh, she sells real estate," said Darcy, "and arranges her own hours."

"Is she married?"

"She was married once for two years to some guy wanting to get landed immigrant status in Canada. She met him in Bosnia when she was twenty. Joy brought him back to Canada with her but as soon as he learned the language and became a Canadian citizen he started to treat her like dirt. They split up. She doesn't have any children and moved into the house across the street after establishing her real estate business. She says her ex moved to Toronto."

Trish peered out the window across the street. There was Joy's blue car sitting in the driveway. Trish cringed at the sight of it. *What could be a motive for Joy to murder Max Weldon? Darcy must be able to connect some loose threads. She must know something. Erica proved not to be a suspect since her DNA didn't match. Yet, she was inheriting some of Max's fortune. Now that's motive,* thought Trish. *Gretchen was at the hospital but it was logistically impossible for her to murder Max.*

"Have you ever noticed a funny odor from Joy?" asked John, "like the smell of marijuana?"

"Well, once Joy came here and said she was experimenting with a new type of perfume and asked if I liked it. I said it smelled like the scent I used to whiff in the apartment building I lived in before Max and I were married. It stunk," said Darcy.

"Joy said she wouldn't wear it anymore but you know she used to smell of it quite often after that. I think she did it just to test my patience and loyalty."

"Darcy," said Trish, "that perfume she said she was wearing and afterwards you smelled more often is the smell of marijuana. Joy smokes pot."

"I know Joy has been a super confidante for me but I don't really know a whole lot about her past life other than her brief marriage. Every time I spill my guts out to her she agrees with me about Max and I don't hear another point of view, just agreement with me; for example, I said that Max wasn't paying me enough support; then she would agree and say you're right. He needs to pay you more support. Don't you think that's a one-sided conversation?"

"You are on the right track. Next time you and Joy meet for tea, see if you can find out what she really thinks about you and Max," said Trish. "John and I will come by for another visit to see how it goes. Thanks for the tea and cookies. We'll be seeing you. Take care and don't worry about your financial situation. Things will turn out all right." Trish and John said their good-byes and left.

After Trish and John left, Darcy drove to the Scotiabank with Max's will in her hand as proof to find out the value of the TFSA and to her surprise she found out that Max's TFSA was worth $200 000. She was relieved at the healthy sum in her name from the will. Max had looked out for her after all. She left the bank and headed back home.

Trish and John pondered their visit with Darcy. They headed for Paul's parked car around the corner but it wasn't there. "Paul must have gone to Tim's. I'll send him a text to get him over here. John, I bet Hadar is Joy's drug dealer."

"I agree," said John. "Do you know when Josie and Charlie are going to visit Joy? She's home now."

"I think Charlie has a late class today, but his plan was to pick up Josie and head over there around 4:30 p.m. which should be anytime now." Paul arrived with coffee and a doughnut. "We'd better head for home, Paul. John and Trish hopped into the car and headed out of the neighborhood. I'll hear more about Charlie and Josie's visit at supper. The CMC will be updated tonight."

Paul, John and Trish shared some of their thoughts about Joy Jensen.

"She knows Hadar and has dealings of some sort with him," said Trish. "A woman was driving Hadar's truck the night of the murder."

"The list from Hadar's trailer looked like a woman's handwriting."

"Joy has blonde hair and from what Charlie said she wasn't too pleasant at the memorial service and when I went to see her she slammed the door in my face."

"And anyone hanging around that creep, Hadar, has to be guilty of something. I think we have enough evidence to obtain a search warrant," said John.

Rob Camden had forewarned Charlie that in order for him to enter Joy's home he'd definitely need two things, a search warrant and an RCMP officer to accompany him.

Rob made a call to Corporal Brown on Charlie's behalf and Brown obtained a search warrant. He accompanied Charlie and Josie to Joy's home in an unmarked police car which he parked a few houses away from Joy's house.

"Charlie, you are such a good friend," whispered Josie. "You listen to me lament and worry about my dad. I'm nervous about Joy's reaction; she might even be hostile."

"Josie, you are going into the home of a possible suspect. Try to stay focused and calm; one more thing, know that we are with Corporal Brown, who has a search warrant," said Charlie.

Joy's rental car was in the driveway as they walked up to the front door and rang the bell. No answer. They rang it again but this time a voice called out, "Who's there?"

"RCMP. We have a search warrant; open up." "Cripes! Just a minute," came Joy's voice.

Corporal Brown waited patiently. Several minutes passed and Brown started to get agitated. "What's taking her so long?"

Just then the door opened and Joy Jensen snubbed them, as Brown presented the search warrant. She glared at Charlie and remembered the nosey, busybody kid. She couldn't forget his questions at the memorial service.

The corporal and Charlie entered the room and started their search. Brown, as a graphologist, one who studies handwriting, looked for samples of Joy's handwriting to compare with the list found in Hadar's trailer. He was pleasantly surprised at the grocery list stuck on the fridge door with a magnet. He slipped the list into his pocket and returned to the living room to see Joy irritated, twiddling her thumbs as she sat on a wooden, dining room chair. Josie sat beside Charlie as Corporal Brown explained the meaning of the search warrant. Brown explained that a search warrant allowed the police to enter a home to look for stolen goods or narcotics. It also could lead to other evidence in the case of a murder. "I'm sorry you made your way here. I have nothing to hide. Go ahead and search."

"You appeared rather agitated at Max's memorial service," said Charlie. "I think you have information that you won't reveal. Why have you become such good friends with Darcy Weldon? Where were you the night of Max Weldon's murder? Did you kill Max Weldon?"

"Questions, questions, questions. Stop the interrogation," said Joy.

"Is this a search warrant or an interrogation? If it's a search warrant, search. If it's an interrogation, then call it that," exclaimed Joy.

Corporal Brown spoke up. "We have every right to question you during our search; so co-operate and answer the questions."

"Darcy, poor helpless thing, has lived a life of hell with that man. She has confided in me as any friend would. We became friends shortly after I moved into the neighborhood five years ago. She's a needy thing full of self-pity and anger towards Max. The night of Max's murder I was visiting a friend in Cornwall. I didn't kill Max Weldon."

CHAPTER 8

As Joy responded, Charlie took a picture of her on his iPhone and Brown studied the two lists, one from the trailer and the grocery list from the kitchen. Immediately he stood up and said, "Joy Jensen, you are under arrest for the murder of Max Weldon." He then took out his handcuffs and cuffed her wrists behind her back. Charlie and Josie were surprised at the instantaneous turn of events. They kept quiet as Corporal Brown escorted Joy out of the house and into the backseat of the unidentified police car.

The same interrogation room where Brown had questioned Hadar was used once again, this time by Joy and Corporal Brown. Charlie, instead of Trish, and Josie stood behind the two-way mirror. This was Brown's domain. He was an expert at breaking people down and getting into their psyche.

Corporal Brown offered Joy Jensen a glass of water before he began. "In my mind I have no doubt that you were the one who murdered Max Weldon. I have specialized training in comparing handwriting samples and I have with me the evidence that will put you away for a long time. You wrote a list for Hadar Whitney of all the items you would need to carry out the perfect crime. You didn't think that he'd be dumb enough to keep that list in his trailer for someone else to find. He had it stashed in a pile of papers where it was found and I have it right here. See? Today at your house I found a sample of your handwriting on a grocery list on your refrigerator. A perfect match for a perfect crime. Fancy that! You'd better start talking because it's downhill from here on in and I want details, even the most minute."

"It will never stand up in court. You are nothing but a bully. Pick on someone else. I won't say another word before my lawyer arrives," said Joy.

"She's going to be a hard nut to crack," said Charlie to Josie behind the two-way mirror.

"As you wish," said Brown, "but remember it all comes out in the end and you'll talk. They always do." Corporal Brown turned off the tape recorder and left the room leaving Joy to ponder her next strategy.

Brown, Charlie, and Josie were in the next room viewing the handcuffed suspect through the two-way mirror. "She'll crack in time. Her lawyer is on her way. Joy called Eliza Lark. Eliza is kind of shady and doesn't have a good rapport with the judges in town," said Brown. "I'm a skilled graphologist. I've solved many cases this way. And if that doesn't work we have a DNA sample on this glass I offered to Joy." The corporal held out a plastic bag with a glass in it. "When the results come back in a few weeks,

I'm confident it will prove to be a match with the blonde hair in the brown wig."

"It's getting late. We should report our whereabouts to our families so they don't worry," said Josie. "I'll text John and you'd better text Trish."

"Ok," said Charlie. They texted: Josie and Charlie are at RCMP headquarters. Will be late. Don't worry.

Finally Joy was placed in a holding cell where Eliza Lark met up with her; so Brown went back to see the kids.

"It all comes out in the end," Brown said. "It's time to go home. Joy will remain in custody and a hearing date will be set. Do you guys need a ride home?"

"Thanks, but I've got my car out front," said Charlie.

Trish, Nana, and Dad were all ears at the supper table when Charlie got home. Josie and John were exuberant too and shared this feeling with their mom. Barb Freeman had news as well. The twins' dad was to be discharged from the hospital and was coming home the next day.

"The case isn't over yet," said Rob Camden. "The judge and trial are still to come."

"Dad, one thing that really bothers me is the motive," said Trish. "We may have proved Joy Jensen is the guilty one, but we don't know why she murdered Max Weldon."

"As Corporal Brown says, it will all come out in the end. Tomorrow's a new day. We have proof today but there is much more to come."

"Can we have the club over for a bit of a celebration tonight? It won't be late. Please, Dad?" begged Trish.

"That's fine. Keep it to a low hum."

The record player was turned down but Beach Boys music was still played. The club knew it was a gathering of festivities; so they came prepared with munchies and pop.

Computer games were popular but mostly the warmth of the group, the success of the day, and the prediction on what was to come in the near future were the prime topics of conversation. The club departed at 10:30 p.m. Trish went to bed shortly after the club left. Charlie played some video games and began rereading an old Hardy Boys mystery of his dad's.

Joy Jensen spent the night in a cell at the RCMP headquarters after Eliza Lark visited her for a couple of hours. The next morning, Eliza arrived at the RCMP station promptly at 9:00 a.m. The secretary at the station handed Eliza the typed copy of Joy's statement and she was admitted into Joy's cell. "Please read this report and sign at the bottom," said Eliza Lark. Joy read it carefully. She knew she had to confess to the murder of Max Weldon and possession of narcotics. However, she was pleased with the wording of the statement, as Joy's confession played heavily on sympathy because of her childhood memories. Joy reflected on what she had confessed to yesterday. *I was twelve-years-old when my alcoholic, gambling father came home one night and said he'd been to the bank to see the manager to extend his mortgage and line of credit. The bank manager refused. He also placed my father on a list of people he planned to force into bankruptcy. Within six months Dad got his notice and was out of a job, and with my mother and three sisters to look after, he couldn't find work. The strain on our family was enormous and we were living on food from the Food Bank and social assistance. The strain on Mom and Dad's marriage was too much. My sisters and I were placed in four different foster homes and Mom and Dad split up. I wasn't allowed any contact with my family and my revenge towards that evil bank manager, Max Weldon, grew and grew. Someday I'd pay him back for what he did to our family. Some day. Well, the time came much later. Max was in his fifties and close to retirement. I saw how he cheated on his wife, the extramarital affairs he had with Erica Peabody and Gretchen Zimmerman. It made me sick. Darcy was clueless about this for a long time until finally she and Max split up. I knew this gave me an opportunity to set the stage for his murder.*

I was looking for some drugs, primarily cocaine, when I heard about Hadar Whitney. He had plenty of stuff to get high on; so I purchased drugs from him on occasion. I asked him if he ever did favors for clients on the side. I told him what I wanted and he supplied me with the items I needed. He also loaned me his truck for the night of the murder. One thing he managed to locate for me that was not collected by the RCMP was a QEH ID badge. When I threw the other items into the washroom garbage can, I had to take the ID badge with my picture on it with me so no one would find my true identity.

Joy shook her head, signed the statement and handed it to Eliza. They waited quietly in the cell until 10:00 a.m. and then left to go to court. In court Judge Campbell decided that Joy was a risk for not appearing for her trial date and thus refused to allow her to leave on bail. She was placed in Sleepy Hollow jail until her trial date.

CHAPTER 9

When Darcy heard that Joy was in jail for the murder of her ex-husband, Max Weldon, she was overcome with emotion. Trish was beside her, comforted her, and listened to her tears and babble.

"She said she was my friend. I trusted her. I confided in her. I didn't want her to murder Max. How could she do such a horrible thing?"

"We really don't know what goes on in another person's head. Joy had a long- lasting bitterness towards Max since childhood. She wanted to stay close to you to arouse the hatred inside of her so she could get her revenge in the end. However, she got caught. Would you like to visit Joy at Sleepy Hollow to get a few of your questions answered?"

"Would you take me there?" asked Darcy.

"I don't have my license but I can go with you in your car if you like."

"Ok. Can we go now?"

They got their jackets and drove the short distance to Sleepy Hollow. Darcy had never been there and neither had Trish. They were met at the gate and were given permission to enter the jail and they were then escorted to Joy's cell.

All of a sudden Darcy got cold feet. What was she going to say? Trish was excited with pent-up energy. She would help Darcy with words to overcome the butterflies in her stomach.

Trish started, "I saw you the night of Max's murder. You were the one who came out of the washroom in Unit 2 and left by way of the staircase. I remember now. You left your disguise in the washroom and a syringe which you used to inject Max with an overdose of morphine. The short, brown-haired wig had a blonde hair in it which belonged to you. We don't have the DNA results back on the water glass, but the police are very confident that your hair and the DNA on the glass you used in the police station will be a match. We also have the handwriting match as evidence.

By this time Darcy was feeling confident to question Joy. "Why, Joy? I trusted you. You were my confidante, my dear friend. Why?"

"I had my own agenda. Having you as a friend just kept me closer and closer to killing Max. I'd listen to you and bite my tongue when you'd say things I already knew in my heart about

Max. I was never a close friend to you, Darcy. You were just a pawn in the path of Max's death. I'm not ashamed of using you; nor was I ashamed of killing him."

Darcy was finished. "I'd like to leave now," she said to Trish. The two of them left the jail and headed for home in silence. Darcy dropped Trish off at her home, said good-bye and continued on to her own place.

The house felt creepy. Max was no longer harassing her and for the first time in her life she felt desolate. No more Joy in her life. She crawled into bed and cried herself to sleep.

CHAPTER 10

The DNA was a match. The month went by quickly and Trish and her mystery club were excited about the results.

Sgt. Freeman's wife, Barb Freeman, had all the papers in order and had Freeman released from the hospital. She also had prescriptions to fill for him. Freeman was a bit sluggish due to the meds, but he knew he had to take them to prevent further lapses and panic attacks. Josie and John were glad to have their dad at home. Rob Camden dropped by for a brief visit. "It's good to have you home again, Coady. The kids certainly missed you. By the way, if you feel up to it, the trial for Joy Jensen and Hadar Whitney is tomorrow at 2 p.m. I plan to be there. Charlie and Trish are going and we'd sure like to have you there."

Freeman's heart started pounding. "I'll call you in the morning and it will depend on my getting a good night's sleep."

Hadar Whitney and Joy Jensen waited for their trial. Hadar was also placed in Sleepy Hollow jail pending the trial date. Today was the day both were to be charged. Eliza Lark was in the courtroom to represent Joy Jensen while Hadar Whitney had no legal representation.

Staff Sgt. Rob Camden picked up Sgt. Freeman at 1:20 p.m. and they headed for the courthouse. Charlie and Trish weren't around anywhere when Rob left the house. *I know the court session was more important to them than any school work. Where could they be?* he thought.

The Camden Mystery Club was seated in the back of the courtroom. They acknowledged Freeman and Rob Camden, who sat a few rows in front of them. To Trish's surprise, Darcy Weldon Erica Peabody, and Gretchen Zimmerman showed up.

Ron Perry, Darcy's lawyer, arrived at 1:55. Ron sat beside Darcy while Erica and Gretchen each sat alone on the other side of the courtroom.

At precisely 2 p.m. Joy and Hadar were escorted to their seats. Eliza Lark sat beside Joy and Hadar sat by himself.

The clerk of the court entered and said, "Please rise." Everyone stood as Judge Campbell entered.

Judge Campbell listened intently as Hadar, Joy, and Eliza spoke. The testimonies were confirmed. Hadar admitted to drug possession and distribution and involvement in the collection of the items for Joy's premeditated murder of Max Weldon. Judge Campbell was harsh on Hadar especially since he was on parole. Eliza got up in Joy's defense. She embellished the story of

Joy's childhood, her anger at her parents' divorce, her emotional upheaval as a teenager and so on. The judge listened but finally had to give Eliza a five-minute wrap- up. Joy took the stand and confessed to the murder of Max Weldon.

Joy was charged with first-degree murder of Max Weldon. Hadar was charged with aiding and abetting Joy's murder as well as drug dealing. Joy received a sentence of twenty-five years with no parole and Hadar a sentence of fifteen years without parole. The court was adjourned.

The Camden Mystery Club cheered. Rob Camden and Coady Freeman shook hands with the club members. Rob Camden invited Sgt. Freeman and family and the whole club over for a celebration, Trish and Charlie, Josie and John Freeman, and Paul.

They didn't need their cell phones tonight. They ordered in Chinese food and played the Beach Boys on the old record player while the Camden Mystery Club rejoiced over the solving of their mystery.

CARI COMPLEX CONVICT

BOOK 2

CAMDEN MYSTERY CLUB SERIES

CHAPTER 1

Trish awoke in a clammy sweat, heart pounding, brilliant visions swirling, deep hot water, a strong arm hold around her neck from a solid body dragging her down and under the water. Down, down, struggling for air…she was not sure of the time. She peered at the clock radio. It was 2:45 a.m. Trying to settle her body reaction, Trish lay there doing yoga breathing exercises, closed her eyes and tried to recover from the nightmare experience. It was no use. Quietly she got up, desperately needing to record the vivid scene in her photographic memory, she reached for her laptop, turned the light on and started to write. By 4:00 a.m. she began to feel drowsy and closed her eyes to drift off into a restless sleep. The alarm was set for 7:00; so she slowly dressed and met her brother, Charlie at the breakfast table.

"Good morning, Trish. Looks like you've had quite a night," said Charlie.

Trish didn't want to let her brother pry into her emotional state. She said, "I've got a project due today. Maybe I'm a bit worried. Where's Dad?"

"I heard him in the shower. He's probably getting ready for work."

"Doesn't matter." Trish absently had breakfast, a piece of toast and a bowl of Cheerios. "Do you have classes today at the university?"

"I'm heading out now." "Will you see Josie tonight?"

"Yah. I'm picking her up after Zumba class to go to the movies."

"What movie are you going to?"

"It's her turn to pick, probably a chick flick. See you later."

Trish wasn't her normal, perky self. She had a heavy heart, a mind full of anxiety, and a nervous, upset stomach. Premonitions were a part of her photograph memory and this one seemed strangely a coincidence to her after- school program. She had a full day of school before she met up with the girls of the Camden Mystery Club at the Cari pool for the Zumba class which was part of her weekly routine. *A drowning at the pool…*she thought. "Dad," jarring herself from her thoughts, as Staff Sergeant Rob Camden appeared for his breakfast,

"are you working on any cases that will allow our mystery club some action?"

"My dear girl, you think too much like a detective.

What are your after school plans?”

“Today I have Zumba. Charlie will take me.” “That's good. I've got to get to work. Have a great day, Trish.”

“You too.”

The Camden's left the house one after the other. Trish, being the last to leave, was responsible for stashing the dishes in the dishwasher and locking up. The bus which took her to East Wiltshire school was on time. As she boarded, her new friend, Ella, greeted her by offering her the empty seat beside her.

“What's up?” asked Ella. “You feeling ok?”

“I'm ok…just a little agitated…didn't get enough sleep. How are you?”

“Good.”

“Are you allowed to come to Zumba tonight?”

Ella nodded. “And you'll never guess what. My parents said I could join your mystery club, that is, if you still want me.”

“Yes, of course. Josie and I are the only girls in the club and we need to recruit new members from time to time. We will be having a meeting tomorrow night.” Trish shuddered at the thought that just maybe there would be a new murder by then. She definitely trusted her premonitions.

"I'm so excited," said Ella eagerly, "going to the pool with you today and then becoming a member of your mystery club tomorrow."

"It's not all fun and games," said Trish. "Solving crimes takes lots of mental work and when you become a member there are things that you are going to learn like how to speak to adults and how to maneuver around cops and stuff like that."

"Oh, it sounds so mysterious. You will help me, won't you?"

"Yah…well, there's the jail…"

Just then the bus turned into the parking lot of the school. The girls left the bus and headed for their homeroom.

The day dragged on and Trish sat idly in her math class pondering after- school activities.

Charlie was taking Josie to the movies after Zumba. The Zumba class was going to be Ella's first time at the pool. *The pool,* thought Trish, *would it be tonight?*

Ella's first time at the pool and maybe a drowning? The end of the day came with the sound of the bell. Trish and Ella raced to the bus.

"Charlie will be driving us to the pool. He's seeing the other girl in the mystery club. Her name is Josie Freeman and she takes Zumba classes as well. I'll introduce you to her when we get there. Dad will be picking us up after class because Charlie and Josie are going to the Cineplex."

"He'll pick me up at my house?" asked Ella.

"Yah, I told him where you live. I'll have a snack and you should have something to eat as well. It's my stop. See you later." Being the first one home gave Trish time to reread her nightmare notes. She sat at the table munching on one of her favorite snacks, revisiting the laptop notes she'd written in the middle of the night.

Charlie, Trish's eighteen-year-old brother, had the use of the old Toyota, a 2005 model, to be exact, on his father's one condition that he drive Trish in and out of Charlottetown on specific occasions. Tonight was one of them.

Charlie had loss interest in the mystery club and only stayed with it because of Josie. He and Josie started dating after her fifteenth birthday and just after the club had solved the Max Weldon murder case. As Charlie's inspiration was new to him, dating Josie, the detective games that he played with his dad and sister had become childish. The Bachelor of Arts degree in sociology at UPEI was the foundation for further studies in criminology. He was preparing himself for real detective work. His focus was on Josie, sports, and parties. He respected his father and begrudgingly drove his sister and her friends to activities.

Ella and the Camdens arrived on time for the exercise class at the Cari Complex. Charlie sauntered off to the hockey rink down the hallway from the pool while the girls entered the locker room. Josie was already in her bathing suit waiting for Trish and her new friend. Quick introductions were made and the girls joined the women and other people in the pool. Zumba was a fast- pace dance class to Spanish music with an instructor dressed in a bright, colorful, fashionable outfit. The leader of the class was fun and kooky but exactly what Trish needed; the loud music and the exercise program filled her with a distraction elevating her mood. She searched the pool and hot tub but all appeared normal. The class with its fast dance movements occupied her entire being. They stayed in the pool until the session was over and it was only then that Trish noticed one of the Zumba girls wandered off to the hot tub to relax after the workout. Josie, Trish and Ella left the area to get changed to meet with Charlie. At the exact moment when the pool was empty and everyone had gone, Trish, fully clothed, proceeded to check on the girl in the hot tub. She was still there. Trish recognized her as a Zumba member but she didn't know her name. She turned to leave when the door to the men's locker room began to move. Trish's hand was pushing on the women's locker room door; simultaneously the doors opened and closed, one opening, the other closing, like ships passing in the night. Neither saw each other. The male walked towards the girl in the hot tub.

"Hello, Rachel," said the mysterious dark- haired, six- foot man, dressed in black swim trunks.

"Do I know you?" asked the girl.

The man slipped into the hot tub beside her, "Oh, you may not know me but I know who you are, Rachel MacInnis, Rufus' daughter."

Rachel stood. The man grabbed her in an arm hold dragging her down, immersing her in the hot water. She struggled but the male was stronger than her. He held on until the life was sucked out of her and the body went limp. The man separated himself from the body and walked out of the pool area. His job was complete. He stealthily walked into the men's locker room, dressed, sent a text and left the Cari Complex. There were no more classes in the pool that day. He had planned it that way.

Early the next morning the lifeguard on duty arrived to find the dead body face down in the hot water. He immediately called 911. Rob got the call from Sgt. Frank Brown and Rob thought he'd better have Mack Pathius turn up at the poolside as well. Trish had heard the ring of the telephone and she awoke to question her dad as to who would be calling at 5:30 in the morning. Rob told her that there was a drowning at the Cari Complex. Trish felt crushed. "I know…I know…I know," she cried. "I had a premonition. Was it a girl in the hot tub?"

"Yes. How did you know Trish?"

"I saw a girl from our Zumba class enter the hot tub just before we left last night. After I got dressed I checked on her and she was still there. I worried all night about her and I just knew something bad was going to happen."

"Do you know her?"

"No. I've seen her at the pool but we've never met."

"I'm to pick up Dr. Pathius and we're to meet Sgt. Brown at the pool. The EMS will be there soon. You must go to school today, Trish. Put it out of your mind as much as possible."

"I feel so responsible. It's my fault that I didn't tell you about my nightmare yesterday. I want to go with you, Dad."

"It's not a pretty sight to see a victim of a drowning and Dr. Pathius will be doing a poolside coroner's review. I insist you stay at home now, get your breakfast, and take the bus to school. I know you've planned a Camden Mystery Club meeting tonight; so you may continue with this event. I've got to get dressed." Rob hugged his daughter and dried her tears on his pajamas.

Staff Sergeant Rob Camden, Dr. Mack Pathius, and Sgt. Frank Brown arrived at the complex within half an hour. The ambulance arrived at the same time. The lifeguard brought the chair lift over to the hot tub and maneuvered it under the body to lift it out of the water. Mack could not do a full report at the poolside but checked for markings on her neck and placed a thermometer into her body to determine the time of death. The temperature of the body matched the temperature of the water which meant the body had been there a long time. "I'd say this girl has been here since last night," said Mack.

The lifeguard spoke, "the last class was Zumba last evening and it ended at 6:30 p.m. There wasn't anyone else in the pool when I shut the lights off and locked up. I didn't see anyone in the hot tub. I checked the visual screen at the supervisor's station and all looked clear. The camera in the pool area doesn't reveal the hot tub; so it was easily missed."

"I'll verify my report with further details once the body is delivered to the morgue," said Pathius.

"Frank, do you have any more to do before the body is removed?" asked Rob. "The EMS are ready when we are finished here."

"There is no ID with the body. Perhaps these flip- flops," as he bent down to pick up the pair, "belong to her and make me think she has a locker in the women's change room," said Brown. "I'll check it out. The emergency services may take over here."

The EMS got their stretcher, covered the body, removed it from the deck, loaded it into the vehicle and off they went.

Rob and Mack exited from the pool area and followed Frank who went ahead to look for a woman's locker that might belong to the victim. "Rob, Mack, check this out," said Frank as he viewed an open locker. "These clothes and kitbag are the only ones here." Carefully he put rubber gloves on and placed the items in a large plastic container.

"We'll take these to headquarters for forensics," said Staff Sergeant Rob. "It's time for a coffee and I'm a little bit peckish. Maybe we can drive through at McDonald's for breakfast on our way, Mack? Frank, we'll meet you at the station."

"Sounds good to me," said Mack.

"I'll pick up something on my way, too," said Frank.

Trish did as her father insisted. She caught the bus and sat with Ella. "Ella, you'll never guess what? The telephone woke me up at 5:30 this morning. Dad got a call about a drowning at the pool."

"But I thought you checked the pool before we left."

"I did but there was one girl from our Zumba class relaxing in the hot tub who wasn't about to leave; so we left and that was when I guess the murder took place."

"Really? You think someone came along and drowned her?"

"I'm positive. We'll have an interesting CMC meeting tonight."

Erica Bradson and Jennifer Gabble were inspecting the contents of the container that Sgt. Brown delivered to the test center. "The victim's name is Rachel MacInnis," said Jennifer. "We have her iPhone here and I can imagine we'll find her address and address book once I crack the iPhone password. It won't take too long. Towel and clothing, shampoo and deodorant, that's about it."

Surprisingly they found evidence of marijuana in several small packets in her kitbag. They also discovered a key on a serpent key chain with an undecipherable code carved into the back of the key.

"What do you make of this, Jen?" asked Erica.

"It looks weird. Maybe it's a school locker key. I'm guessing the victim is about sixteen and probably goes to high school.

There aren't many high schools in Charlottetown. It looks like our victim, Rachel, is dealing in some weed.

We'll get Sgt. Brown to check it out."

Erica said, "Marijuana isn't the only thing this girl is up to. Look at this." She pulled out a baggie filled with small packets of white powder and another bag of pills. "It looks like cocaine or heroin or even fentanyl. Holy cow, she might be a major drug dealer in the city."

"We'd better keep this information to ourselves, or we may have someone, you know who, inspecting us." No sooner were the words spoken when Corporal Kurt Lewis poked his head into the lab. "I heard you gals were examining the stuff found in the locker room at the pool this morning. Did you find any leads?"

"We are checking her kitbag now," said Jennifer. The two exchanged a brief oh- no-not-Kurt glance. "Nothing much to go on, where's Sgt. Brown?"

"You gals better not withhold information from me. I have every right to work this case and I'm a corporal; so you'd better start sharing your searches," said Lewis sulkily.

There was no way they'd spill the beans to Kurt Lewis. He was an egotistical, macho man whose arrogance and free-flowing mouth would get them in trouble.

"Sorry Cpl. Lewis. Nothing to report at this time," said Jennifer. "Now if you'll excuse us we'd like to continue our work. Have a nice day." Lewis insulted left in a huff.

"Now let's run this iPhone through some computer tests. Here we go, Erica." The results came up on the laptop. "Oh my gosh, here is her address and her whole territory of users with email addresses and cell numbers. We hit the jackpot!"

Dr. Mack Pathius was at the Queen Elizabeth Hospital morgue investigating the body of Rachel MacInnis. Cpl. Lewis peered over his shoulder, "What have you got here, Mack?"

"It's none of your business. I report to Sgt. Frank Brown and I will not amuse you with my investigation. You'll have to be informed by one of your superiors. Now scram."

"I'll be back and I'll have proof of my job description that I have the right to your report." Lewis stomped off not knowing where to go next. He returned to his office and began searching his job description.

Staff Sergeant Rob Camden was in a conference with detective Frank Brown perusing the information accumulated thus far on the drowning case. The victim was Rachel MacInnis, a sixteen-year-old girl with kitbag contents insinuating that she was heavily involved in the drug scene on Prince Edward Island. "Frank, let's look into her family history. My God, Charlie is eighteen and I can't imagine him ever knowing anything about the drugs on the street.

How did this girl get involved in such a criminal activity? You'd better include Lewis in this investigation. I want to hear from you by the end of the day."

"Ok. I'm not use to having Lewis tag along but if you insist, I will."

"I insist for your protection and remember he has your old job."

"Very well," said Frank as he departed from Rob's office.

Frank walked down the hall and into Kurt's office. "Hey, Kurt do you want to get involved in this drowning case?"

"It's about time I was asked to get involved. What's up?"

"We're going to pay a visit to the victim's mother. Do you think you can handle this?"

"Yes, of course."

"Well, let's check out this address," said Frank as he pushed a piece of paper into Kurt's hand.

The two detectives left the RCMP station and headed towards Hathaway Drive.

CHAPTER 2

The members of the Camden Mystery Club arrived for seven, all except Paul who was usually late. At 7:20 Paul landed with nacho chips and dip in one hand, his Tim's coffee in the other and his smart phone in his back pocket. Introductions were made in a pleasant way to include Ella as a new member of the club. Trish opened the meeting with the news of the drowning at the Cari Complex.

"I had a premonition about the drowning of a girl the other night which came true early this morning when the lifeguard at the pool found a girl's body in the hot tub. Our dad told us her name was Rachel MacInnis and she was sixteen-years- old. Detectives Sgt. Brown and Cpl. Lewis went to her house to question Rachel's family this afternoon."

"Do we have an address?" asked Paul as he dipped and munched on his nachos.

"Yes. She lived on Hathaway Drive. Paul, you can check out the full address."

"Already done. G. MacInnis 35 Hathaway Drive."

"Tomorrow, if no one objects, I plan to take Ella on a visit to her house," said Trish.

"What have you scrounged up about Rachel and her family so far?" asked John.

"I overheard dad on the phone with detective, Sgt. Brown. He said something about Rachel living with her mother but I couldn't make sense of the rest of the conversation."

"What do you want me to do?" asked Josie.

"Why don't you, John, and Charlie check out the school she belongs to. Hathaway Drive, Paul, is it in the Colonel Gray High district?"

Paul checked his cell. "Yes it is, but it's the weekend and they can't check out the school until Monday. Why don't you text us with your information once you and Ella pay the mother your visit. Then we'll see where that leads us."

"Everyone in agreement?" asked Trish. "Yes," they said.

"Charlie, will you drive Ella and me to Hathaway Drive tomorrow morning?"

"Only if you pay for the gas. I'm not your taxi service, Trish."

"Fine. How much?"

"From Cornwall to and from Charlottetown will cost you 10 dollars," said Charlie. "By the way, Josie and I are going to a basketball game at UPEI in the morning; so you'll have to work around our schedule."

"Brother, you are a royal pain. Ella, can you contribute to the fund?"

"I have five dollars at home," said Ella. "Well I have five, too. It's a deal, Charlie."

"Ok. The game starts at 10:30. Josie and I will drop you girls off at 10 a.m. You can walk back to the gym and meet us there to get a drive home. We'll pick you up, Ella, at 9:45. See you tomorrow," said Charlie.

The meeting was adjourned. Charlie drove Josie and John home.

The next morning the girls paid Charlie and got in for the drive to town. Ella whispered, "I'm nervous." Trish squeezed Ella's hand to reassure her. Fifteen minutes later the two girls stood outside 35 Hathaway Drive.

"Oh, I see it's an apartment building," exclaimed Trish. "Thanks, Charlie. We'll see you at the game."

Trish reviewed the questions and protocol for Ella with Rachel's mother. "Don't worry, Ella. I'll lead the way and you can follow me and ask a question when you feel comfortable."

"I'll be ok once I'm there."

The girls found the apartment and knocked on the door. A middle- aged woman answered it.

"Hello, Mrs. MacInnis?" asked Trish. She nodded. "We are sorry for your loss. We saw your daughter at the Cari Complex Zumba class the other night. We don't know her but we belong to a mystery club and would like to ask you a few questions about her."

"Mystery club? I don't have to answer to a kid's mystery club when I've just lost the most important person in my life. The RCMP was here yesterday and I told them everything I know."

The grieving woman was just about to slam the door when Trish said, "My dad is the head of the RCMP in Charlottetown. He believes our mystery club is a valuable part of his investigations."

This piqued the woman's interest. "Do you know who was here yesterday and what is your father's name?"

"My dad's name is Staff Sergeant Rob Camden and he sent detectives Sgt. Frank Brown and Corporal Kurt Lewis to question you yesterday."

"Does your dad know you are here at my door this morning?"

"Well he wouldn't be surprised to find out we are here," said Trish. "The information his detectives received from you yesterday just might not be the same as what we'd hear from you today. Please let us come in. My name is Trish Camden and this is my friend, Ella Omoto."

"My name is Gloria MacInnis. I'm very upset; so you will excuse me if I don't answer all of your questions. Come in." The girls entered the small apartment. The curtains were closed and the living room felt like death. Gloria didn't offer a drink; instead she sat down in a comfy chair with a Kleenex box in her hands. She motioned the girls to sit on the couch. Trish began with her usual question, "Do you know why anyone would want to murder your daughter?"

Gloria shivered at the question and then said, "I think there is a possibility that some Mafia would want to see Rachel dead. Have you heard of the Mafia?"

"Yes," said Trish.

"Rachel is her father's daughter and he belongs to an organized crime underworld. I divorced him when he'd fill Rachel with lots of images of fashion and materialistic things… things I couldn't afford to give her. She had expensive tastes… he said he had ways for her to be able to buy her own car and have anything she wanted. I suspected his ways were through the criminal drug trade and I lived in fear of this happening to Rachel and feared for my own life as well."

"Does Rachel's dad live in PEI?" asked Trish. "Well, that's a good question. He comes and goes like the wind. I never see him but I know Rachel has. My suspicions are that Rufus has had Rachel dealing drugs at the schools here in town."

Trish made a photographic mental note of Rachel's father's name.

Ella blurted, "Can we see Rachel's bedroom?"

"Oh no, the detectives said not to let anyone into the room. It's off limits." Ella felt embarrassed.

Trish picked up on this and said, "That's quite understandable. We don't need to see her room. Do you have any family here?"

"No. My brother, Wayne, is arriving tonight from Vancouver."

"If your suspicions are correct, do you know who is supplying Rachel's drugs?"

"I'm terrified of the whole underground world. I chose to raise her in a more positive, happy, moral life. I just think she followed her dad's lifestyle and not mine." Gloria started to cry.

"We'd better go," said Trish, "we're so very sorry for your loss."

Ella and Trish saw their way out.

When they hit the street they texted a brief message to the club members. Something Trish knew but Ella didn't know was that Hadar Whitney, the local drug dealer, was in prison; so the underworld had already filled his position. Trish sent a more personal text to Paul to look into the drug trade hierarchy. The girls hiked their way back to the UPEI gym. On the way Ella said, "You were great in there, Trish. I felt so self-conscious and embarrassed when Mrs. MacInnis answered me with, "no, you can't see her bedroom."

"Don't beat yourself up, Ella. It was your first time at an interrogation. It will become easier. Just think Rachel may be a drug dealer. This could become a scary case. I think dad will withhold information to protect us."

The two pondered the interview as they walked toward the UPEI campus. Trish received a text from Paul. It said, "I've got important info for u. Will drop by in pm to discuss."

"Trish, who was the text from?"

"Uh…uh, it was from Paul. He has information for me but wouldn't put it in a text. Says he'll drop by this afternoon. He may be onto something big and dangerous."

"This sounds frightening," said Ella. *Maybe we are at the tip of the iceberg, and Paul has uncovered a series of drug dealers,* thought Trish.

"Oh well, we'll just have to wait and see. Don't be frightened about something you don't know, Ella." The remainder of the walk they hiked in silence. They arrived at the gym as the basketball game was over. 96-88 for UPEI. Josie spied them first. Charlie and Josie met up with the girls and headed for the parking lot. "What a great game." said Charlie. "Did you guys get anywhere with Rachel's mom?"

"We did indeed," answered Trish. "Sounds like Rachel's dad is in the thick of things in the drug trade here in Prince Edward Island and he's replaced Hadar Whitney with a middle person. I texted the others and I received a text from Paul that he wishes to meet up this afternoon. Peculiarly he wouldn't text the info that he found."

"Who is Hadar Whitney?" asked Ella.

"Hadar Whitney was a drug dealer here last year when he was sentenced and placed in jail."

Ella nodded. "Did the Camden Mystery Club have anything to do with the arrest?"

"One could say that," smiled Trish.

"You're at it again, Trish. John and I will support you in any way that we can," said Josie.

They approached the Toyota, climbed in and were off to Cornwall. Ella and Josie were dropped off; then Trish and Charlie made their way home for lunch.

"Charlie, you will get involved in this case, won't you?"

"Maybe. We'll see what Paul has to say this afternoon."

The siblings arrived at an empty house. They remembered how lucky they had been to have their nana stay with them while dad was convalescing from his heart attack. Nana had always been there for the kids while they were growing up and lunch would have been prepared for them. Now that dad had recovered and was back to work, the teens were fairly independent; so Nana had suggested it was time for her to make a break and live on her own. Trish thought how vacant the house felt. Charlie and Trish made sandwiches, munched on potato chips, and guzzled orange juice.

Charlie sent a text to Paul while Trish texted their dad as usual by habit to let him know they were at home. Paul appeared at their doorstep shortly after one.

It surprised them that he arrived so early. Paul entered nibbling on a box of chocolate- covered raisins. "What's up, Paul?" asked Trish.

The three of them went to the basement where the club always met and Paul got right to the point.

"You Trish, asked me to check on the hierarchy of the drug trade and boy, did I ever find some interesting yet fearful information. When Hadar went to prison last year a new person by the name of Renko Hemlock came to PEI as a replacement. That's not all. He reports directly to a Rufus MacInnis who is in charge of the crime scene in all of eastern Canada. The next member of the chain is the head honcho, Gondola Favio."

The CMC is unable to research the Mafia in depth because of the potential danger to them and their families. As an aside to the reader here is some background information on Gondola Favio.

Gondola Favio is the Don of the Mafia in Canada. He lives a life of luxury in a high-rise apartment in downtown Toronto. He is at the peak of a pyramid of Mafia persons working as drug dealers, murderers, gamblers, sleazy, dishonest lawyers, and evil low life. He wasn't always in this high-level position, as he had started out lying to teachers in elementary school when asked to pass in assignments which were never done. You see, his home life was a shambles with a cheating, gambling, alcoholic father and a prostitute for a mother. He never had a normal childhood. At age seven, he would be sent out of his dilapidated apartment stinking with the disgusting scents of weed, cigarettes, alcohol and filth to find his dad at a bar or casino and bring him home. His mother cooked processed and sometimes contaminating, unhealthy foods to feed Gondola which caused him to put on weight as an adolescent. Gondola never experienced love in its pure, unconditional form. He was whacked as a teenager by his parents when using foul language. Gondola thought his life was hell. He promised he would work for himself and at age sixteen he started dealing drugs for a pimp of his mother's.

Gradually he began to show leadership qualities in the Mafia underground and took on larger territories doing everything from stealing, dealing, and murder. He was ruthless but never got caught. The opportunity arose for him to serve as the assistant to the Don of the Mafia. At age twenty-seven he sought out a luxurious apartment of his own and surrounded himself with expensive material goods and beautiful women. He had connections throughout the country and filled positions that became available when a Mafia person was captured. The police never touched him, as he was always protected by the underworld.

Then one day the Don of Canada was murdered and this left Gondola in charge of the entire Mafia in Canada.

Gondola was deceitful, jealous, and vengeful, on one side and yet on the other he kept business very private while enjoying good food, and loose women. His lifestyle was unlike his childhood. He was in charge. He always went to church on Sundays. He kept a pure character to uphold yet had a whole country's Mafia working for him. Drug shipments from the US and Mexico were handled by some of his Mafia men. He made contact through texts when he was dealing. The drugs were smuggled into Canada from Mexico and the US and distributed from there by a Canadian port to various locations around the nation. The drugs that were smuggled were cocaine, heroin, and fentanyl.

"Gee whiz, Trish. You've gotten into a real kettle of fish," said Charlie as he looked at his wide-eyed sister. "Yes, I will get involved."

"I can see why you couldn't put it into a text message. Rufus MacInnis is Rachel's dad. It makes sense that Gloria, Rachel's mom, said, 'He comes and goes like the wind.' He has a large area to cover but Rufus MacInnis must have other local dealers in eastern Canada," said Trish.

"Well, Renko Hemlock is the dealer in our province," said Paul.

"That's right; so Rachel would be getting supplies from him. She's the victim and yet we wouldn't have her killed by another drug dealer in the hierarchy, would we?"

Paul said, "No. And Rufus wouldn't want her murdered, as she was his own daughter. The direct order to kill her must have come from Gondola himself. Maybe Rachel was wanting out of the whole Mafia crime world and her knowledge of the drug trafficking made her a loose end. Gondola could have had her murdered by a hired assassin."

CHAPTER 3

"**I** found hemorrhaging in the lungs which is a sign of sheer force causing death to the victim," said Dr. Mack Pathius. "I also found organs in the body that were at a high temperature which help to indicate the time of death between 6:45 p.m. and 7:00 p.m. just after the pool emptied from the last class of the day."

"The pool was locked at 7:00 p.m.; so the killer must have fled just after the drowning," said Frank Brown. "Do you have anything else?"

"If you look closely at our victim, you will notice bruising on her neck. I took samples of skin from her tissue to see if the killer left any skin cells of his own. I will send a sample of cells which I scraped off the body to Erica and Jennifer. They'll have to ship them off to Halifax for a DNA analysis. The killer was approximately six feet tall and very strong. I checked the body especially the head for some measure of bodily fluid such as saliva or perspiration from the killer but I didn't find any. That's all. Hopefully the DNA on the skin cells will help your case, Frank."

"Thanks, Mack. You always do a thorough examination. I'll head back to the lab to see what the girls have found."

Jennifer Gabble was busy itemizing the contents of Rachel's kitbag. Erica Bradson had her head down peering into a microscope and looking at the skin tissue that Dr. Pathius had sent to them. She was about to speak when Sgt. Brown arrived. "I think we've got something here. I see two very different skin cells, one from the victim and the other from the assailant I'll send this sample to the forensics lab in Halifax for DNA analysis," said Erica.

"Great," said Brown. "How about the kitbag, anything of interest in there?"

"Show him, Jen. Show him what you found."

"We found the victim's iPhone and cracked the password to find names and email addresses and some of the drugs they require, cocaine, heroin, and even fentanyl. It is a long list. We also found a key of some sort on this serpent keychain. It looks like the key to a locker. We checked the code on the back of it but it is quite damaged. It appears to be a series of letters in lower case. Magnified the code looks like 'r-u-f-r-m- a' which doesn't make sense to us."

"Is there a locker number on the key?" asked Brown. "Yes. The number on the other side is 141," said Erica.

"I'll take the key and the iPhone and run it by Rob.

You've done a great job, girls."

"What should we say if Cpl. Lewis comes back? We wanted to talk to you first. We respect your opinions."

"Thanks. Just send him to me and I'll handle him.

Keep up the good work."

Frank Brown knew he had no choice but to involve Lewis in the detective operation. He couldn't go to the Staff Sergeant before engaging Kurt Lewis in the case. It was protocol…the way things were done at the RCMP station. The iPhone and key were evidence that was needed to be discussed with Lewis. The drugs were another thing. Frank didn't like this chain of command but he was the sergeant, since Coady Freeman had retired, and he had to speak with the next in line to his corporal detective. He thought he'd review the iPhone first, come up with a strategy, and then go to Lewis. He went back to his office and closed the door. If he was lucky, Kurt would be reviewing the session they'd had with Gloria MacInnis.

The iPhone was a running record of users in the greater Charlottetown area. This was a miracle for Brown and would surely lead him to the next contact in the drug underworld. He knew Hadar Whitney was in prison and his position in the chain of drug dealing would've been filled immediately. Rachel's death created a new position in the dealer world.

He thought about Gloria MacInnis' statement about trying to have a better life for her daughter and the dad she had that was never there. Gloria mentioned her ex's name was Rufus and he was connected to the Mafia cartel. Rufus was to blame for Rachel's lifestyle and her death according to Gloria's sentiments.

CHAPTER 4

Rufus MacInnis ached over his daughter's death. He thought that this would never happen and yet knew that it was part of the criminal world. Why wouldn't Gondola let her go if she wanted out? Why did she have to be eliminated? He had known for some time that Rachel was in danger as she worked the schools in Charlottetown. The last time he saw her was three weeks ago when they met at Victoria Park for a conversation.

"Dad, I want to give up my responsibilities to the Mafia," said Rachel.

"I'm not hearing you, Rachel. This is your life now and you belong to the greater business of the cartel. Do you know what happens to one who wants to get out? It is a very dangerous option. You are only a pawn in the Mafia. Gondola and Renko Hemlock will fill your boots in a flash. If you mention you want to get out, then you are as good as dead."

"You have an important job with the Mafia, Dad. You control all the comings and goings of the entire Atlantic region of Canada. The Mafia doesn't need me. I'm just a girl in the greater scheme of things. Why can't Gondola dismiss me and allow me to go ahead with my life?"

"I will talk to him but I warn you the Mafia doesn't like loose ends. If someone wants out, they usually get snuffed out for good. I don't want that to happen to you."

"Have you always been connected with the Mafia, Dad?"

"I started as a teenager just like you. They provided me with a home, a car, and money to live a comfortable life. I married your mother without her ever knowing my connections with the cartel. After you were born, your mother started asking me questions about my employment and how I came by the money I received. It was then when you were eight-years-old that I told her the truth. She was devastated. She swore to leave me and never return. I couldn't give you up just like that. Gloria wanted a better, honest life for you; so she got an apartment and I would visit you from time to time."

"Why did you make my life so dependent on money? I remember you teaching me about the drug business when I was thirteen. You made it sound so glorious. I could have anything I wanted, anything I wished for myself monetarily. I got hooked and for the past three years I've been working for you and Gondola."

"Do not speak of him so casually. He has many connections and I am afraid for your life."

"You've taught me to be resilient. I can take care of myself. I'm a big girl now, Dad. Good-bye."

Rufus reflected on the last conversation he'd had with his daughter. She was so brave yet stupidly courageous. Rufus sat on the side of his bed with hands covering his face. He could not go to the funeral. He was so deeply immersed in the damn Mafia.

Gondola Favio as the Mafia head Don could choose to execute anyone who would betray his business; he had ways of dealing with them. Rachel MacInnis was a liability and he couldn't have that. It didn't matter that she was Rufus' daughter. He protected himself by contracts with those who did the dirty work for him. Evil was his middle name. He made his call to his assassin. He assigned the contract and texted, "Let me know when the job's done."

CHAPTER 5

Seth Ewell landed at the Charlottetown Airport on an Air Canada Jazz flight from Toronto. His assignment was clear. He had been emailed a photo but that was all. It was crucial to find the victim, stalk her unnoticed for a few days to see her daily routines, then eliminate her. Rachel MacInnis was an attractive girl, wore expensive clothes, and drove a Toyota Camry. He observed all of this within the first day in Prince Edward Island. He found her address and cell phone number with ease. He was the best assassin in all of North America. He kept his eyes and ears on the street. He knew her high school, viewed her making drug deals and followed her to the Cari Complex for her Zumba class. All of this information was collected undetected. He spoke as little as possible to anyone. He was on a mission. The time factor for the entire researching of data and elimination of the victim only took five days, in and out quick without leaving a trail. He didn't need to get into her life and he knew how to spy and disappear. The worse scenario would be if someone recognized him; however, he was confident that that was highly unlikely. He was in control of the situation. It was his decision to carry out the murder by a method of his choice. He had disguises to use if needed. During the collection of data he needed to enquire about the camera at the poolside. Under disguise he went to the Cari Complex and discovered a noteworthy tidbit of important information. The camera on the pool only showed coverage of the swimmers in the pool. The hot tub was never on the screen. It was also invisible on the front desk screen. What an easy target. His victim went to the class every week at the same time. He found out that on Thursdays there wasn't another group afterwards; so the pool was vacated immediately and Rachel always entered the hot tub for a few minutes after class. *The perfect sight for a perfect murder,* he thought. He'd leave Charlottetown on a night flight to Toronto.

CHAPTER 6

Sgt. Frank Brown and Cpl. Kurt Lewis decided to check out the mysterious key on the serpent keychain. Did it belong to a locker in the Colonel Gray High School? It was Monday morning and they set off for the school. Frank knew they would need permission from the office to inspect a locker in the hallway.

"Good morning, my name is Sgt. Frank Brown and this is Cpl. Kurt Lewis. We are investigating a murder which took place last Thursday evening of a former student, Rachel MacInnis. We found this key with her belongings and would like to test it out on locker 141. Could you please escort us to this particular locker?"

"One moment please," said the secretary. "I'll notify the principal to go with you."

The secretary returned with Mr. George Bastain and introduced the officers and their purpose.

Mr. Bastain said, "A murder? Rachel MacInnis, you say? I'm curious to see the contents of the locker as well. She's had a bad reputation from what I've heard. I only know the gossip from the other students but it's usually true, what they say, I mean." The three of them left the office and set off to find locker 141. The corridors were long and had lockers on both sides of the hallway. They turned left, then right, then turned right again and finally came to the appropriate locker. Brown took out the key and tried it. The principal and RCMP officers weren't surprised that the locker opened on the first try. However, they were surprised at the contents.

" Wow," said Lewis. "Look at all this drug paraphernalia."

"Be careful, Kurt, we must not touch the evidence without rubber gloves," said Brown. "Please take some pictures with your iPhone before we start to disassemble things."

George Bastain was flabbergasted by the evidence at the scene before his eyes. He noticed rolled up five dollar bills, white powder on textbooks, cards with residue left on them, a purse, baggies of weed, a scale, rolling papers for snorting cocaine, lighters, Visine and Clear Eyes, perfume, a glass pipe, and some surgical needles. He also spotted some Tictac cases with pills and some baggies with white powder in them. "All of this in my school, I'm speechless."

"Well, we will be busy here for a while and we don't want to keep you from doing your job; so we'll collect everything in plastic bags and see ourselves out," said Sgt. Brown.

Lewis was busy taking pictures from different angles when the principal made his exit. "Please let me know if you need me for anything…anything," said Mr. Bastain. He returned to his office and wrote a memo to staff re drug use in Colonel Gray High (FYI).

Frank and Lewis began disassembling the contents of the locker, placing anything of evidence in plastic bags. Frank kept a close eye on Lewis to check that he was following protocol and labelling Rachel's belongings in separate categories. They completed their task within an hour, left the locker open, and swung by the office to say their work was finished. They thanked the principal for his assistance and made their way to the RCMP vehicle. They stashed all evidence in the trunk and returned to the station.

"Do you have any idea what the letters stand for on the opposite side of the key?" asked Lewis.

"I'm not sure. The r-u-f I believe stands for Rachel's father, Rufus, but the last part of the code would be a guess. Maybe the r-m-a stands for Rachel and the m and a for MacInnis. Just a guess though."

"How did you figure that out?" "It's just how my deciphering brain works. Of course, I'm not sure but for now the code doesn't help the case and probably its purpose is identification, that's all. Our intention is to get these exhibits back to the forensics team."

"They're not that helpful. Jennifer and Erica have something up their sleeves and they wouldn't share anything with me," said Lewis with self- pity. I don't think they like me. What's wrong with me? I'm a corporal, and they tell you everything yet reject me. What gives?"

"They've dealt with me a lot longer than you. You are going to have to earn their respect. They don't want you to speak up as if you are a know-it- all."

"Well I'm not going to take crap from them."

"You better not come on strong. If you want them to share their data, then watch how I deliver myself and learn. I've never had a problem with them. Be prepared to take notes when we arrive."

The officers unloaded the car and took the drugs and drug paraphernalia to the lab where they met up with Jennifer and Erica. "Here's an early Christmas present," said Brown. "We are delivering the remains of the Rachel MacInnis locker found at Colonel Gray High."

Lewis spoke, "High...get it? Colonel Gray High... as in marijuana high...get it?"

"Yah…we get it," groaned Jennifer.

"We've bagged and labelled everything to make your job a little easier. If you have any questions, I'll be in my office," said Frank.

"Um…um, you can see me in my office as well. We work as a team and teamwork is so important; so I just want to be consulted when you have any questions," said Kurt.

"Lewis was helpful too," said Frank. "He got some great shots of the locker and its contents."

"Gotcha," said Jen. Erica dismissed them with a little wave as they exited the lab.

CHAPTER 7

Trish called the Camden Mystery Club meeting to order. "Charlie and I had a very informative meeting with Paul this afternoon and will discuss this when Paul arrives. All I'll say is that Paul has cracked open the hierarchy of drug dealing in our province and in our country."

"I think he's come across knowledge of significance," said Charlie as he glanced at Josie.

The doorbell rang. Paul arrived with a pizza.

"I'm a bit late but you know my hunger pangs take priority."

"The group is waiting for you downstairs," said John. "I'll be right there."

Paul kicked off his sneakers and followed John down into the club den. The den itself was plastered with posters of successful cases they had read about, an old record player where they usually spun old Beach Boys records of Dad's, an old lamp with a floral design lamp shade, a chalk board, and an array of comfortable chairs and a sofa.

The members of the club were all waiting expectantly for Paul's news. Once Paul put down his pizza, he began to speak. "I was looking at some dark sites illegally today and came up with some drug-related names and positions these people have in the hierarchy of drug trafficking. As you know, the victim, Rachel MacInnis, was drowned in the pool last Thursday night. We found out there is a replacement dealer here on PEI taking over from Hadar Whitney's business and his name is Renko Hemlock. He was a direct supplier to our victim.

But you'll never guess who is next in line up the ladder of command; it is Rufus MacInnis, Rachel's dad. Here comes the conflict. Would Rufus really want his daughter murdered? I doubt that. I dug a little further into these websites and found out our Rufus reports directly to a man by the name of Gondola Favio. Gondola is the head Mafia leader in all of Canada and he resides in Toronto. He is responsible for shipments of drugs into the country from Mexico. He could have easily hired an assassin to kill Rachel. Take a minute and look at the names and order of command they have as I write their names on the chalkboard."

"How are we supposed to find a hired assassin when he probably slipped in and out of PEI without our knowing?" asked John.

"A very good question," said Charlie, "Trish, do you have any idea where we should go from here?"

"I'm stretching my brain to the night of the murder/drowning. I had a premonition early in the morning on Thursday. I wrote it down as best as I could remember. When the girls left the pool that evening, I saw a girl in the hot tub which sent shivers up and down my spine. So after I was dressed I went back to the poolside and no one was in the pool area except for the girl. As I was leaving I had a sixth sense that someone was coming out of the men's locker room. I didn't see a face; therefore, it's not much to go on. Well, we could try to relive the actual scene. I'll pretend to be the victim while Charlie, you pretend to drag me under the water. How would you keep me from getting away?"

"I'd use an arm hold with my right arm around your neck like this," as he demonstrated his grip with an arm hold on Trish.

"That's good. Now the only part of the killer's body touching the victim's body is where Rachel's neck is held tightly by the killer's arm hold. I would think that the forensics team might find skin cells from the victim's neck that may have been mixed with the killer's arm hold," said Trish. "If the coroner is doing his job he would have samples of these cells taken to the forensics lab to have the DNA checked. If this is the case, it takes three to four weeks to get DNA results from the lab in Halifax, Nova Scotia."

"You sound so professional," said Ella, "but what do we do for the next few weeks?"

"We've come up with this snag before; so let's brainstorm what we can do?" asked Trish.

"We've visited Gloria MacInnis; maybe we can talk about that," said Ella.

"Gloria tried to give her daughter a better life, but money was more important than love to Rachel. It was too late for her to get out; she was in so deep," said Trish.

"Paul, how about telling us how you gained all your information?" asked Josie.

"Sorry, Josie, I don't want to get anyone else into those particular websites meant for adults over the age of eighteen. We can talk about the fact that with the death of Rachel MacInnis a new distributer will be needed at the school level. We can talk about the RCMP involvement. Trish and Charlie can discuss the investigation with their dad. John and Josie can discuss Hadar and his replacement, Renko, with their retired dad, Sgt. Freeman," said Paul.

"It sounds like we've places to go to keep us busy.

Let me talk to Sgt. Brown and Cpl. Lewis," said Trish, "and I'll take Ella with me. Are there any objections?"

"That's your connection and don't forget to speak with your father as well," said Paul.

"For sure. I guess that's all for now. We won't need another meeting until more evidence appears. Meeting adjourned."

"Hey, Dad," said Trish after the club was dismissed. "What's going on at the RCMP station with Rachel's belongings and cell phone?"

"How do you know she had a cell phone?"

"Oh, come on Dad, everyone has some sort of electronic device nowadays."

"Trish, I want you to stay out of this murder investigation."

"I can't. Our mystery club has already delved in pretty far and I am designated as the one to get the low- down from you."

"All I'll say is that Sgt. Brown and Cpl. Lewis have cleaned out a school locker that belonged to the victim and found drugs and drug paraphernalia. They have met the victim's mother."

"Oh, you mean Gloria MacInnis?" "How did…oh never mind…yes, Gloria MacInnis."

"How did Dr. Pathius' report come back? Did he send some skin cells to forensics and did they send them to Halifax for DNA analysis?"

"Trish…you've got ESP or a very orderly mystery crime mind."

"Like father…like daughter," said Trish with a giggle. "The funeral for Rachel is on Wednesday afternoon.

I expect you to stay in school and not skip out."

"I promise you Dad, I will not go to the funeral; besides, the killer won't be there. He's long gone."

"I suspect you're right about that one. Maybe I should be asking you for information."

"Check out our chalkboard in the basement and if you have any questions, I'll be free to answer from what we've got. Did anyone crack open Rachel's cell phone yet?"

Rob nodded as he took the stairs to the basement. "Oh, Trish, you're into something very dangerous. How did you get these drug contact names?"

"It's just part of our investigation procedure, Dad," said Trish loudly as dad was still in the basement.

Rob appeared back in the kitchen. "Sgt. Brown and Cpl. Lewis and the forensics team are the only ones who have access to the cell phone data. Sorry, I can't divulge this information."

"That's ok, Dad because our club doesn't need it. We'll search in other ways. Don't worry about us, Dad. It would be nice if you could keep me posted on further developments in this case."

"Please, Trish, don't put yourself into any risky situations."

"Ok, Dad. Well, I'm doing a little more homework on the case. See you in the morning."

CHAPTER 8

Jennifer was printing off the list of names found on Rachel's iPhone. Erica was getting data organized on her computer. Sgt. Brown walked in just in time to receive the computer printout from Jen. "Thanks," he said. "I'll inspect these phone records." He was in a hurry to get back to his office before Lewis cornered him. Frank wanted to peruse them alone without queries from the corporal. He wanted some aspect of the investigation to himself, at least for a little while. It was just so annoying to have Lewis breathing down his neck and whining about everything. He closed his office door and sat at the desk.

The phone records revealed very specific details to him. A call from her dad, Rufus MacInnis, three weeks ago was of utmost importance. Several calls from a Renko Hemlock looked suspicious. Was Renko Hemlock her supplier? He knew the name. Calls to and from him were on many evenings from 8 p.m. to 10 p.m. Frank knew Rufus was the one overseeing the Atlantic region of drug suppliers. He also knew Renko was a PEI supplier who was replacing Hadar. That didn't concern him for the moment. Perhaps Renko was directly dealing with Rachel.

Suddenly a knock came at the door. Rob poked his head around the door. "You've got phone records, I hear," he said. "May I come in?"

"Of course I'll share them with you. Come in. I've noticed a few interesting calls. Several from Renko Hemlock and one from Rufus MacInnis, Rachel's dad, placed about three weeks ago. He's the one I'd like to snag. We don't have an address for him, do we?" asked Brown.

"It's highly unlikely his ex-wife, Gloria, could pressure him out of hiding. I'd sure like to seize him, too. I must tell you my kids and their mystery club have a hierarchy of dealers on the blackboard in the basement of my house. They have Renko Hemlock as a supplier for Rachel, and Rufus as Hemlock's Atlantic region Mafia man. At the top of the board they have Gondola Favio as nationwide drug importer directly from Mexico."

"Sounds like they have done some research," said Frank.

"Yes, but it worries me to think they may be in deeper than I'd like."

"I think we should intercept calls coming in on this phone," said Frank as he held the cell belonging to Rachel.

"It's unlikely there will be any calls from dealers. But there may be important calls from users. Yes, keep this phone under surveillance. Have you seen Kurt Lewis today?"

"I haven't seen him."

"Tell him I want to see him when he arrives." "Will do."

Staff Sergeant Rob went back to his office. Frank wondered where the heck Lewis was. It was already half past ten. He sent a text to Lewis without a response. At eleven, Lewis appeared looking all smug about his whereabouts. "It's 11:00 a.m. and where the heck have you been?" asked Brown in a seething voice. "Rob wants to see you immediately."

"As a matter of fact, I want to see him, too," Kurt Lewis smiled self- righteously. He left Brown and went to Rob's office. "I hear you want to see me?"

"To start with you are late. Where have you been? I wanted to send you and Frank over to Gloria MacInnis' apartment."

"Already done," said Kurt.

"What do you mean?" asked Rob.

"I've already been there and collected vital information about the address of Rufus MacInnis."

"You mean you went alone? Against RCMP protocol? You idiot."

"You wouldn't say that if you knew what I know." Rob was fuming. His blood pressure was rising.

Trying to calm himself down he said, "You deliberately went against our protocol. Now go see Frank and rectify the situation. I don't want to hear anything you have to say before you and 'your partner' make a decision together. Go!"

Lewis was dismissed. His face was flushed. As Lewis shuffled down the hall and into Sgt. Frank Brown's office, Brown noticed Kurt's demeanor had changed since his arrival. "You look as if you've been banished. What's up?"

Kurt didn't want to hear Frank's 'I-told-you-so' lecture; so all he did was pass him a piece of paper. "Here…it might be of some use to us."

Frank looked at the paper. "Whose address is this?"

"When our victim was drowned, her father, Rufus, went to see his ex- wife, Gloria at her apartment. He shared with her his sadness and placed this piece of paper in her hand if she should ever need it. He knew she was a loner and he recklessly gave her his address and cell number. Opening the palm of his hand he revealed the cell number which was written in ink. Gloria thought it might be of value to us. She had no intentions of using this information as she long ago wanted her privacy from the cartel."

"You twit. I understand why you look so sheepish. Rob lectured you about RCMP protocol. When are you going to get it through that thick skull of yours…you have to follow protocol;

you and I must go together on RCMP matters. That cell number might help us solve the mystery of the hired assassin or at least help drag Rufus into our investigation. Let's test this address together. Are you ready, dimwit?"

"Yes, I am partner. We'll stick to each other like glue."

"Whatever. Come on,"said Brown.

The two detectives informed Rob and headed for the parking lot. They made their way downtown to 54 Eagle Street, Apt. #3.

CHAPTER 9

Rufus sent a text message to Renko. It read: *New shipment to arrive at 11 p.m. on Thursday; pick up delivery at bus station.*

Renko was reliable to pick up Rufus' shipments. He filled Rachel's vacancy with a new dealer for the high schools within a day. He was the middle man, so to speak and he knew the ins and outs of the drug business. The RCMP knew his whereabouts too, and were prepared to arrest him on drug trafficking charges; however, what the RCMP didn't know was his connection to Rufus MacInnis and that this was the drug lord they wanted to nail.

Sgt. Brown and Cpl. Lewis knew through Kurt's conversation with Gloria that Rufus had a huge role in the Mafia. He reported directly to the don. It was the don, Gondola, however, who had hired the assassin who killed his daughter which to Rufus was unforgivable. Rufus had mixed feelings. He was torn inside, eaten up with emotional pain. He couldn't retire. No one retired from the cartel without being snuffed out; so he continued to follow his role as deliverer of illegal substances to all the eastern Canadian cities and towns. He had a round about way of shipping to keep the police off his trail. He received his supplies directly from Mexico but they didn't go to his Charlottetown address; rather they went to a small village in Nova Scotia by boat. From there they were delivered by bus to Charlottetown, Prince Edward Island, and other Atlantic destinations. This diversion kept his address safe. No one knew his real address except for Gloria. She would keep his location safe, or so he thought.

Frank and Kurt arrived at the address that Gloria gave them. They waited outside the rundown apartment building before someone coming into the building opened the door and let them in. The detectives found apartment number three and banged on the door.

Rufus opened the door. He was a professional and didn't let little things bother him. "Yes, can I help you?" he asked as he stood there looking at two policemen in uniform.

"Are you Rufus MacInnis?" "Who wants to know?"

"We are detectives with the RCMP and we are investigating the murder of a young girl at the Cari Complex. Do you know this girl?" They held up a picture of Rachel that Gloria had given them.

"I'm sorry I don't know her," he lied as a shot of pain reached his heart.

"Are you Rufus MacInnis?" "Yes."

"You must come with us down to the station for questioning."

"I've nothing to hide."

Kurt had his handcuffs in his hands and cuffed Rufus. Brown led the way for Lewis and the suspect to follow. Lewis shoved Rufus into the back seat of the police car. They drove to the station and placed Rufus in the interview room. The room was equipped with a video camera and an audio tape to collect data. Frank took the lead in the questioning while Lewis observed from the next room through the two-way mirror.

"We know you are involved in the drug trade. This picture, as he held up the picture of Rachel again was one of the drug dealers at the high school level. We have information that leads us to believe she is your own daughter. She was found in the hot tub at the Cari Complex drowned by someone who may work for the drug cartel."

"I've been to see your ex-wife. She says you've been to see her and gave her your address and cell number. Rachel was her daughter and all we have to do is take a DNA swab to prove you are her biological father. But more importantly, we are delving into the drugs on the streets in PEI."

"I want to see my lawyer."

"I'm not finished with you yet. Get your lawyer; then we'll talk," said Brown as he left the room.

Rufus was taken to another room where he phoned his lawyer, Thomas Stretch. The detectives knew the line of questioning would be more difficult with a lawyer present. They knew they could prove Rachel was Rufus' daughter but they didn't have any way of proving Rufus' dealings with the Mafia.

"Let's not forget the phone call Rufus made to Rachel on her cell three weeks ago. This is proof that they knew each other," said Frank, "I almost overlooked this detail. To go any further in this investigation we're going to need a search warrant."

"That's right," said Kurt.

"Let's post what we do know. Rachel, our victim, is Gloria's daughter. Gloria was married to Rufus MacInnis but is presently divorced. Gloria has identified Rufus.

Rachel was the drug dealer for Charlottetown high schools. We've retrieved samples of cocaine, heroin, and fentanyl found in her kitbag and school locker. Renko Hemlock has replaced Hadar Whitney as the primary suspect for bringing illegal substances into PEI. He is the supplier to several dealers in the province; all we know for sure is his connection to Rachel. We have phone calls traced to Rachel's cell confirming their dealings and meeting places. We also have the phone message we collected from the victim's phone made by Rufus a few weeks ago. We have enough information to bring Renko Hemlock in for questioning but we need to get two search warrants, one for Renko and the other for Rufus. We have reason to believe they are heavily connected to the Mafia in Canada," said Frank. "Rufus is in custody pending the arrival of his lawyer."

"We won't get too far once he has his lawyer at his side," said Lewis.

"You're right about that one."

The two detectives set off for the court house to get two search warrants from a judge. It was a procedure which didn't take too long. Frank and Kurt located Renko Hemlock's address at the RCMP station and proceeded to his Charlottetown apartment. Brown hammered on the door saying, "Police. We have a search warrant. Open up."

Renko fled to the window and was about to jump out of the two-storey building when the door was shot open and Lewis grabbed Renko, threw him onto the floor, and placed him in handcuffs. "You're not leaving so soon. We're taking you for a ride to the police station. First, we're going to take a good look around your apartment."

Detective Brown prodded carefully throughout the apartment finding ample drugs and drug equipment. "We've got this one. Renko Hemlock, you are under arrest for possession of illegal drugs for the purpose of supplying in the province of Prince Edward Island."

Lewis shoved Renko into a corner of the room.

Brown took the opportunity to take pictures of the crime scene. Then he sent a text to headquarters to send a couple of RCMP officers to clean up the apartment.

"Who's your supplier? How do you accumulate this crap?" demanded Lewis as he seized a bag full of small packets of white powder.

"Kurt, don't put your fingerprints on this stuff. Remember to use your gloves. Do I have to remind you of all procedures?" asked Frank irritably.

"So sorry. I forgot."

"I think you'd forget your head if it wasn't attached to your body."

The RCMP officers arrived and the detectives secured Renko in the back seat of the car and drove back to the station. They took him to the interrogation room where Rufus had been a couple of hours before. The video camera and audio tape were turned on. Frank began the cross-examination while Lewis watched from the next room behind the two-way mirror. Frank questioned Hemlock persistently about his sources of illegal substances until Renko finally cracked and made a slight confession. "I don't know my provider personally. We've never met. My supplies come from Nova Scotia and I pick up a shipment at the bus station in Charlottetown."

"I see. Show me your phone," said Brown. Renko hesitated, "Why?"

"Just give me the phone."

Reluctantly Renko passed it to Frank. "Now write your password on this," as Frank placed a piece of paper and a pen in front of Renko. "Go ahead and make it right. I'll know if you're giving me a fake password and you'll feel pain if you antagonize my good nature."

Renko Hemlock was trapped. The pen quivered as he wrote his password on the paper and passed it to Sgt. Brown.

"You stay here as I look into the phone numbers on your phone." Frank left the room, told Lewis to keep an eye on him, and strode off to see Jennifer and Erica in the lab where they could check the phone records. They retrieved a long list of calls from Rachel and Renko. The list also revealed some calls from the same number Rufus used to call his daughter. Frank was pleased with the results as they linked Renko, Rachel, and Rufus together in the drug business on Prince Edward Island.

CHAPTER 10

The weeks went by quickly while the Camden's and the RCMP waited for the DNA results from Halifax, Nova Scotia. Rufus' cell phone was confiscated by Lewis when Rufus was in the interviewing room and once again was reprimanded by Brown. "Lack of protocol," said Frank. However, the good news was the phone numbers linked Rufus to Gondola Favio, Renko, and Rachel. Finally the DNA results came in and the skin cells on the body of Rachel were mixed with those of another. The DNA check list of criminals in Canada didn't match the skin cells on the victim. Trish was disappointed when her father came home and told her the news. Immediately Trish said, "Widen the data base to include not only Canada but the United States and Mexico as well."

"That's quite an expectation, Trish," said Rob Camden.

"A hired assassin could be anywhere by now and I feel a premonition about this, Dad."

"Ok, Trish. I'll extend the search to the U.S. and Mexico. Not only because you are my daughter but because you have a keen sixth sense." He also thought the drugs could be smuggled into Canada via Mexico or the USA.

Gondola received Seth Ewell's text: *The Rufus girl has been taken care of; the job is finished.* Gondola sent a text to Rufus. It read: *Rachel has been taken care of; your status is safe; do not seek revenge; all will continue as is.*

Rufus wanted revenge. His life was desperate. He was so secretive; so in the depths of the Mafia underworld. He wanted a better life; yet, saw his future as a pawn to Gondola and his Mafia connections. He remembered his only meeting with Gondola about five years ago. At that meeting Gondola confided the three alias' he had for his assassin. He never mentioned it again but Rufus knew how easily he could be dead. Here he was at the RCMP station awaiting his lawyer, Thomas Stretch. He thought of the alias' for Gondola's assassin. In Canada his alias was Seth Ewell; in the USA he was known as Ricardo Vanse, and in Mexico he was known as Pedro Ragu. Pedro was his original name and his homeland was Mexico. This assassin had three different passports, one for each country. Rufus continued to ponder what choices he had: to live on the inside of the Mafia and continue his work with them yet feel like death warmed over; spill the beans to the RCMP and go to jail or be snuffed; or take a new identity and leave the continent forever.

Rufus was deep in thought when Thomas Stretch arrived with a briefcase and was ushered into the holding cell where

Rufus was being kept. Thomas was a seasoned lawyer and one who worked with Mafia- related cases.

"Hello, I'm your lawyer, Thomas Stretch. We shall work out this case together concealing issues that are irrelevant. What have you told the police so far?"

"I have denied recognition of my daughter when a picture of her was shown to me. I have said nothing about the drug trade and my involvement. They have my iPhone which connects me to Rachel, my daughter, Renko Hemlock, Gondola Favio and Gloria MacInnis, my ex-wife."

"Well, it sounds as if we've got a hole from which to dig ourselves out. Did you give the iPhone willingly or was it confiscated without permission?"

"They had a search warrant; so I gave it to one of them."

"I should ask you what you see as a reasonable truth in your testimony to the RCMP. May I ask you to deliver a statement that will hold up in court?" asked Stretch.

"I haven't any loophole. I guess I'm prepared to issue a statement to the police. They have the right to take a DNA sample in their search warrant. This will prove I am the victim's father." Thomas wrote down this information. "I don't want to rat on the Mafia or I'll get whacked. I'm in a real conundrum."

"Phone records can and will be used in court. Are you aware of this?" asked Thomas.

"Yes. What are you suggesting…I confess?"

"I think the best avenue for you is to plead guilty and make a solid statement to the judge at the hearing; however, if you do this the Mafia will surely get you in the end and you'll be a sitting duck; or for your own protection I suggest you take my advice and disappear. I can arrange for you to take on a new identity and send you off to a European country where you can live without fear every time you walk out the door. I know Gondola would get you if you stay here on Prince Edward Island. I can easily make you fade away."

"How can I get released from this police station?" asked Rufus.

"Leave it to me and sign the statement placing you in my custody. I've done this before and I can do it again."

"With your guidance I will take the latter option. Get me out of here forever. I will choose a new identity."

"I will work on this proposal and have you out of here within forty-eight hours." Thomas stood and shook Rufus' hand. "I'll be back soon. Be prepared."

Trish and Ella were doing homework together but were mostly chatting about the mystery club. They found out from

Trish's dad that Rufus and Renko were in holding cells at the RCMP station. The girls wanted to go to the RCMP headquarters but Rob said a definite no. How could the Camden Mystery Club get involved in this crime?

Rob knew the chalkboard in the basement had the hierarchy of drug dealers in the Mafia and worried that the kids might do something foolish which could endanger the case, or worse, affect their safety. He had just found out that the DNA from the skin cells provided a match to a Pedro Ragu in Mexico.

Brown and Lewis flew to Mexico on an evening flight to work on the case with the Policia Federal Ministerial, the Mexican Federal Police in hopes of finding Pedro and escort him back to Canada to face trial for the murder of Rachel MacInnis.

Gondola in his empire-condo in Toronto heard through Thomas Stretch that Rufus and Renko were in custody in PEI. He sent a text to Thomas. "Delay RCMP custody of Rufus and Renko." When Thomas received this text, he was perplexed. Stretch wanted to grant Rufus his freedom, yet he was faithful to the Mafia and Gondola. Now who was in a conundrum? Thomas decided he'd support Rufus and prepare him with a new identity despite Gondola's request. As far as Renko was concerned he'd leave him in custody. What Gondola didn't know wouldn't hurt him. Besides, Gondola owed Thomas a huge favor and Gondola knew it.

Rufus met Thomas two days later. "Is everything ready?" he asked.

"Yes. Here is your new passport, your ticket to Rome, and five thousand dollars to get you started off," said Thomas. "Now sign this paper and practice your new name, George Walton. A taxi is waiting out front. I will escort you to the taxi and take you to the airport where I will leave you."

Rob Camden came out of his office at the exact moment when Thomas and Rufus were about to leave. "Where are you taking Rufus?" he asked.

"Here is a custody agreement which permits me custody of Rufus MacInnis until the hearing," said Thomas as he passed the legal letter to the Staff Sergeant.

"You are to keep him in your own home until the hearing?" asked Rob suspiciously.

"That's the way the legal system works, Camden," said Thomas.

"Well, we'll be keeping an eye out on you, too."

Thomas and Rufus walked past the head officer of the RCMP and exited the station where a taxi was waiting for them. "A piece of cake," whispered Thomas to Rufus. "To the airport," he said to the driver.

CHAPTER 11

Sgt. Frank Brown and Cpl. Lewis reached their destination within twenty - four hours and went directly to the Federal Ministerial Police in the head office of Mexico City. Here they learned that Pedro Ragu, alias Seth Ewell and alias Ricardo Vanse was a farmer. Agent Jose Rodriguez explained to the RCMP officers that Pedro lived on a plantation with large fields where he grew barley, coca plants, and opium poppies. These fields and the buildings on the property were heavily guarded and fenced off with tall barbed-wire barriers. If the detectives were going to try and pay a visit to Pedro then they needed his help.

"We're here to arrest Pedro Ragu. He's murdered a girl in Canada," said Sgt. Brown.

"We keep him in close proximity at all times," said Rodriguez. "He travels all over the country.

"We'd like to help you with your arrest. Please allow me to guide you to his headquarters. We've been stalking his comings and goings for a long time and whatever you have on his head will surely be a benefit to us as well. We should take an unmarked car. Please come this way."

The Mexican policeman escorted Frank and Kurt to the vehicle.

"Dad, what's going on with your detectives? You haven't said anything to me about the case in days," said Trish. "How come you're not informing me of any news?"

"Trish, I don't want to have you stick your neck out on this particular case. It's too dangerous. Frank and Lewis are in Mexico working the case from there."

"In Mexico? And you never told me? When did they leave?"

"They flew out yesterday and are en route to the assassin's headquarters as we speak."

"An assassin has a headquarters?" asked Trish. "It's complicated, Trish."

"Well, please explain it for me. Does the assassin have a name or names?"

"Yes. The DNA match came from a Pedro Ragu in Mexico. We found out that he has three names or aliases. Here in Canada he is Seth Ewell, in the USA he is Ricardo Vanse, and in Mexico he is Pedro Ragu. He lives in Mexico."

"So you've kept this all to yourself, Dad. I'm disappointed in you not even letting me know about the DNA match. I was the one to suggest broadening the search to include all of North America. I'm having a Camden Mystery Club meeting here tonight to fill in the gaps in the case with the other members of the group. Josie, John, Ella, Paul and Charlie have been in the dark about this case for quite a while. I can't believe you've even kept me in the dark."

"Sorry, Trish. There are names on the blackboard downstairs that shouldn't be known by any of your club and it's my job as your father to protect you from Mafia connections. There, I said it. I wanted to keep your nose out of police business especially my soon-to-be- sixteen- year-old daughter."

Trish began to calm down and in doing so, she put her arms around her father. "You're forgiven, Dad. May I please have the club over tonight to play catch up on the case?"

"Yes, on one condition; you erase the names off the chalkboard," said Rob.

"It's a done deal. Thanks, Dad. One more thing, could you speak to the club for a couple of minutes to guide us in our detective search?"

"I will do that but you'll have to obey the RCMP procedures."

"Ok. I'll text the club now. See you later."

That evening the youth appeared at the Camden house; even Paul was on time with his munchies. They all remembered the last night they got together when Paul had written the three names on the blackboard which had spelled out the hierarchy of the Mafia in Canada. The board was blank. Once the initial gabbing settled down, Trish spoke, "I've asked Dad to come down to our meeting to give us a sense of direction for our sleuthing. Dad, you can come down now," Trish hollered up to the kitchen above.

"Hi young detectives, I think you've gotten into a real snake pit. I can only help by reminding you of RCMP protocol and request you to ask permission from me for any of your research. This is a very dangerous case and I don't want any of you hurt. I spoke with Trish this afternoon and told her the Mafia hierarchy on the blackboard was accurate but must be erased from the board and from your minds. A DNA match was found and Sgt. Brown and Cpl. Lewis are in Mexico following a lead. Two of the names you had on the board were presently in holding cells at the police station. A local lawyer has taken one of them in his custody."

Whispering around the room was followed by Charlie's question, "Can you give us the name of this lawyer?"

"He's well-known in Charlottetown. I won't reveal his name. Sorry that's all I can say for now. Don't go snooping in this case. I'll let you continue with your meeting." Rob went back upstairs and left the club to mull over his information.

It was Paul that spoke first. "He's well- known and he has a criminal in custody. That sounds fishy to me. What lawyer would put their life in such a position?"

"A crooked lawyer if you ask me," said Charlie.

"I agree," said Trish. "Paul, google search lawyers in Charlottetown and any unusual cases they have had in the past ten years."

The others were speculating when Paul interrupted, "I've got a lawyer by the name of Thomas Stretch, who works privately and took a suspect to his home two years ago and when it came time for the trial the suspect had disappeared. Now that looks very suspicious."

"We must act on this right away," blurted Trish. "Do you have a business address for this Stretch guy?"

"Yeah, his business is 560 Royal Drive in Charlottetown. Someone should pay him a visit; what does the club think?" asked Paul.

"I was thinking about the two names on the board. Which ones were at the RCMP station? It must be Renko and Rufus. Gondola wouldn't be on the island. Rufus is Rachel's father; so I sense the two of them were in the station. Of course, we should send someone to visit Thomas Stretch. I feel it's not my turn to hog all the interviews; so I would suggest Charlie and Paul to follow through with a visit to Royal Drive," said Trish.

"Now she's getting thoughtful," said Charlie in a derogatory way. "Paul and I can handle this. After the meeting we can discuss our strategy and the time of our visit to Mr. Stretch's office."

"That's good for me," said Paul. "Trish, are you in an intuitive mood? Tell us your thoughts."

"Yes! It appears to me that the guy Stretch has in custody might be able to escape before the hearing and another thing, would Thomas Stretch really take a Mafia guy to his own home to protect him? Hardly. This may be a Mafia loophole and Stretch is a dirty lawyer."

The others agreed with Trish's suspicions.

"Dad wasn't thinking straight to allow the Mafia man, probably Rufus, out of the holding cell and let Stretch take him to his own home. Maybe he was taking him somewhere else like to the airport," said Charlie getting a little more enthused over the case.

"Do you think it is Rufus that left the station with Stretch?" asked Josie.

"Stretch wouldn't think Renko was as significant a pawn as the next one up the ladder. Rufus lost his daughter, Gondola had her murdered, and now he wants to take revenge on the whole Mafia cartel. He wants out, I think, and Stretch is providing the way. That is my hypothesis," said Charlie.

"I agree," said Trish, "How did they get by Dad?" "He probably had a signed document, something lawyers always have with them," said Charlie.

"I think Stretch wanted to give Rufus a fresh start in another country using a fake passport. Gondola would be enraged," said Trish.

"Hey, that's a strong possibility, Trish," said John. "That would make sense," said Josie.

"Well, I think Charlie and Paul will have an interesting discussion with Thomas Stretch at a scheduled meeting in the not-too-distant future," said John.

"We'll meet back here after they find out what's happening with Rufus MacInnis," said Trish.

"Meeting adjourned."

CHAPTER 12

Jose drove the unmarked car through the city and out into the local farmlands. The desert-like landscape was home to Pedro and Jose, and both knew of each other. They acted like a cat and mouse chase Jose being the cat always trying to catch the mouse, Pedro. Maybe this time he'd catch him with two detectives from Canada and his search warrant. He wondered if only he could nab Pedro at his main headquarters where illegal drugs were being produced.

Jose slowed down as he turned onto a rugged, hard- packed, clay road. "We'll be there soon," he said to the drowsy cops. Immediately Frank became alert.

"We're almost there, Kurt," said Frank. He looked at his partner who was sound asleep. "Wake up," he grumbled in a louder voice.

Lewis shook his head and said, "Are we almost there?"

"Yes," the two in the front seat, said simultaneously. "What's our plan of action?" Frank asked Jose. "Pedro lives behind locked, guarded gates. He also has hidden cameras surrounding the property. It has always been tricky trying to get onto the compound but today I feel lucky; besides, I have a search warrant and an exceptional plan that I want to propose. There is a small, deserted landing strip a couple of miles from here. While you were resting, I radioed head office and requested a chopper with extra ammunition to pick us up at this landing strip. There it is, see? There is the helicopter."

The two detectives realized they had come down a slow grade of a hill in this scrubby desert land into an open flat land and eyed the runway where Jose was pointing. Lewis spied the helicopter. We're heading for the landing strip, right?"

"Yes," said the two in front. "Gotcha," said Lewis.

"My plan is to take Pedro's men by surprise by entering the headquarters by landing the helicopter inside the compound. With the extra ammo and smoke bombs we can hopefully daze the guards and get Pedro to come out of hiding."

"Whoopee," Lewis said.

"Don't mind him," said Frank. "This is a very serious situation and we don't want to botch it up."

Jose continued. "We want to seize the ring leader but we also want to shut down the entire drug manufacturing plant. This is a huge undertaking."

Sgt. Brown sent a text to Rob Camden. Rob texted back. The three in the car were getting pumped up. This was going to be a real sting. They arrived at the landing strip where there was an old, rickety hangar. Everything around looked deserted except for a small private plane parked beside the runway. The detectives got out and stretched their legs. They poked around the hangar and checked the locked airplane. "Looks like Pedro's private plane, probably for drug trafficking around the country," said Jose.

Frank looked at Lewis who was doing stretches and getting ready for a jog. "Go ahead and have a run but make it snappy."

"Thanks, boss," said Lewis. "I'll be back soon." "He doesn't have such a bad idea," said Jose. "You've been cooped up since yesterday flying and driving. By getting the old body working it seems as if he's got things figured out."

"I'm not one for jogging but I will do some stretches and wait here," said Brown.

A few minutes later Kurt returned energized. "We should check on the ammunition, weapons and smoke bombs. Everything appears ready. I'll ask the pilot if he's ready to take off," said Jose.

"Let's get a move on," said the detectives.

The three squished their way into the four-seater helicopter and the pilot started it up. Up and away from the landing strip they flew over desert scrub land until they began to see fields of grass. From the height of the helicopter they couldn't distinguish the vegetation. They flew over a peak and saw for the first time the complex in front of them. The buildings were substantial. "There is no landing spot on the grounds." As he pointed, "Over there is the dwelling of your criminal. We'll land in the front yard," said Jose.

The helicopter hovered above the building which created havoc with the workers in the area. Three men exited the house and started to shoot at the helicopter. The chopper landed and the police started to fire back. It was a sight of chaos and confusion. More men came from another building and opened fire. "There's our guy," said Jose. By now the only protection the detectives had was behind the helicopter. "I'm going after Pedro. You two create a diversion," shouted Jose. Frank threw a smoke bomb. Jose struggled to get to Pedro. Lewis shot a man in the leg. Then he injured two more. Frank was covering Jose with gunfire. Jose seized Pedro. He cuffed him and dragged him to the chopper. The smoke dissipated and the gunfire stopped. Jose shoved Pedro into the helicopter. "We have a search warrant," said Jose. He chained Pedro to a seat inside. "Sgt. Brown and Cpl. Lewis, come with me." He nodded to the pilot to stay on guard. The three detectives proceeded to one of the buildings. They found a vast amount of drug manufacturing. One lone worker fired at the police. Lewis shot and injured him. It was over. Jose radioed his force to send ambulances and a narcotics team to Pedro's headquarters.

The detectives searched the grounds and Pedro's house. They found a woman huddled in a corner who only spoke Spanish. Jose spoke to her asking where Pedro's passports were. She was frightened. She motioned to a painting on the wall. Frank examined behind the painting and found a safe. They were all there - three passports, three identities. Back at the Federal Ministerial Police station a swab of DNA was taken from Pedro's mouth. It was immediately sent to the Mexican forensics lab in Mexico City. Jose got the DNA results. Frank sent the results to the RCMP station in PEI. It was a match. They had proof of Rachel's killer who was in cuffs and ready to be transported back to Prince Edward Island.

Rob said, "Trish, I thought you'd like to know Sgt. Brown and Cpl. Lewis have Seth Ewell, I mean, Pedro Ragu in custody and are returning him to face the charge of murder of Rachel MacInnis."

"That's great, Dad. The Mystery Club will like to hear the news. I'll text them right away. What's going to happen to Gondola, though? And when will they get home?"

"Gondola, I'm afraid, hasn't a charge on his head; maybe next time. For now we will have the assassin. They arrive home the day after tomorrow."

CHAPTER 13

Trish didn't tell her father about the visit that Paul and Charlie made to Thomas Stretch's office. She had waited patiently for her brother to fill her in about the location of Rufus MacInnis. When Charlie got home, Trish practically pounced on him for information. "How was your meeting with Thomas Stretch? Where is Rufus MacInnis?"

"Can you wait a minute," said Charlie. "Paul and I went to Thomas' office and met him. He is one sleazy lawyer. We asked him about Rufus MacInnis and said we heard a rumor that he was living with him. Thomas looked surprised. He never heard of such a ridiculous rumor and didn't even know a Rufus MacInnis."

"He was lying," said Trish.

"Of course, but he wasn't the most amiable person. Told us to get lost and never come back. Even though we were suspicious, we left and went home. Another kettle of fish we're not going to find out about."

"Dad told us about the release document Thomas showed Dad when he departed the RCMP station with Rufus."

"I think he's definitely a dirty lawyer; probably works for the Mafia on occasion. I think he had a new identity for Rufus and sent him away. Somehow we'll never know."

"Well, we can rest our minds about Rufus ever turning up again. He wanted to get out of Gondola's control and start a new life. Losing his only daughter, Rachel, and knowing the ins and outs of the Mafia and the assassin, Seth Ewell or Pedro Ragu must have been a heavy burden. A new life must have sounded pretty good," said Trish.

"When do Brown and Lewis bring the assassin home?"

"In a couple of days," said Trish. "You know, I think Ella and I should make a visit to Gloria MacInnis to let her know the assassin has been captured and is on the way back to PEI to be charged with murder."

"I think that's a very good idea, but you'd better wait until Seth is back. You don't want something to go haywire in transport of the criminal."

"That's a good idea. Have you heard anything about Renko Hemlock?" asked Trish.

"Not much. Dad said Renko would be kept in a holding cell at the RCMP station until his hearing next week," said Charlie.

"The hearing for Pedro, alias Seth, will be next week as well. Quite a coincidence, don't you think?"

"Yah, you and your coincidences and premonitions have really had quite a case. I imagine Seth will request a lawyer to represent him."

"I wouldn't be surprised if Thomas Stretch is his lawyer," said Trish.

"Yah," said Charlie.

"He is legal representation for all Mafia-related cases."

"We'll see. I'm off. See you at the CMC meeting."

Renko Hemlock had his preliminary hearing with a provincial judge who charged him with drug trafficking. He pleaded not guilty and was sent to Sleepy Hollow jail until his trial by jury in July.

Sgt. Brown and Cpl. Lewis landed home with Pedro/ Seth without a glitch. Seth hired Thomas Stretch as his legal defense. He was charged with first- degree murder and placed in Sleepy Hollow jail as well until his trial by jury in July. Thomas met Seth there. "Don't worry," said Thomas Stretch.

"They have my DNA. Doesn't that make me guilty?" asked Seth/Pedro.

"Yes, you're right. The extradition laws between Canada and Mexico require that you be tried by a judge and no jury will be present. Your only evidence of the murder crime is the DNA sample which will hold up in court."

"So why do I need a lawyer if you can't get me freed?" "You were the one who contacted me for help," said Thomas.

"Well, I don't need help from you anymore," said Seth. "You are fired."

"Fine." Thomas Stretch got up from his chair and left without another word. Pedro/Seth knew he was guilty and that he'd have to face the judge on his own. He returned to his cell at Sleepy Hollow.

Renko's trial came and he was sentenced to ten years in prison on the trafficking of illegal drugs and was sent to the Atlantic Institution in Renous, New Brunswick, which is a maximum- security prison. Seth appeared before a judge and was charged with first-degree murder and was sentenced to life at the same prison in New Brunswick.

Rob Camden came home on that day to share the news with Trish and Charlie. "DNA samples work every time in the justice system."

"Wow! That's great news," said Trish. "I'd like to visit Gloria MacInnis to explain how the judge made his decision. Is it ok if I take Ella over to Gloria's? Charlie, will you drive us to 35 Hathaway Drive?"

"Yes, you can go and take Ella with you. Charlie, you will take the girls, won't you?" asked Rob.

"Yah, but they have to text the club and have a special party tonight," said Charlie.

"That's the best idea I've heard from you in a long time, Charlie," said Trish. "Dad, can you spare a few dollars for the party munchies?"

"Ok, Trish. Remember to keep the party subdued."

Gloria was satisfied to hear the murderer was going to prison. She offered tea and cookies to the girls. Ella and Trish sat for a while with Gloria. "Please drop by anytime. I'd like the company," said Gloria, as the girls got ready to leave.

"We won't forget you, Gloria. Take care," said Trish.

Party time in the basement of the Camden household was awesome. Paul brought food and so did the twins. Everyone was in an elevated mood with the closing of the case. The music was lively. Charlie and Josie cuddled on the sofa while the others danced and ate through the night. Rob gave them just so much freedom. Lights out and guests home at eleven o'clock.

MURDER AT THE CONFEDERATION CENTRE

BOOK 3

CAMDEN MYSTERY CLUB SERIES

CHAPTER 1

Trish whispered into Ella's ear, "Isn't Gilbert so handsome? What do you think, Ella?"

"Ssh, Trish. I love him. It's almost over." The rest of the mystery club was all quietly engaged in the theatre watching the last number in the musical, "Anne of Green Gables," being performed at the Confederation Centre Main Stage Theatre in Charlottetown. Ella Omoto, the newest member of the Camden Mystery Club had only dreamed of this very moment. As the song ended, tears of joy and exuberance filled her eyes and heart. Trish and Ella joined the audience in a standing ovation as the cast took their bows.

"I knew you'd like it," said Trish.

"I read the book in school back in Japan but this performance brought the whole story to life and to think my parents bought tickets for the whole mystery club to attend this last performance of the season. I could sit through the whole show again."

Hiroki and Akiko Omoto were standing a few rows back and were happy that their daughter was settling into life on Prince Edward Island. As the audience began to filter out of the theatre, they met up with the club members. Akiko shed tears of joy as she, too, read the book in Japan. When they caught up with the club, Hiroki said to his daughter, "How did you enjoy the show? Don't forget the mystery club will meet the cast over in Memorial Hall in a few minutes. We should proceed to that place now."

"Thank you, Father; the show was beautiful. I loved it so much."

Hiroki had immigrated to PEI last year and started up an investment business. He spoke very good English as he had dealt with financial partners in many countries and English was the common language used. Akiko, on the other hand, was taking English classes in Charlottetown and was improving gradually. They were happy they made the move to get away from Japan and the problems they'd experienced there. They made the decision to move to improve the quality of life for their daughter, Ayumi, and suggested she pick a new Canadian name and she chose Ella. Trish Camden became a welcome guest at the Omoto home as she helped Ella with so many island cultures and mystery activities.

John and Josie, the Freeman twins, Paul and Charlie, all followed the Omoto's into Memorial Hall with Trish and Ella in the lead. Hiroki outdid himself as he had the cast and club catered to with a long table covered in a white table cloth and a huge array of food prepared for the occasion. This was a party for the end-of-season cast and Hiroki arranged the entire event to include Trish's mystery club members. Hiroki and Akiko would do anything for their only daughter. This was just one of the ways they showed their love for her.

The cast was there and Ella and Trish saw the handsome Gilbert helping himself to a plate of food from the table. Their hearts pounded as they wanted to meet him. Trish took the lead and Ella followed. "Hello, Gilbert," said Trish. "We really loved your performance."

"Well, I'm not Gilbert anymore for this year anyway. My name is Dan Redmond. I'm glad you liked the show. I heard you are part of a mystery club that sounds like fun. You're…?"

"My name is Trish Camden and this is my friend, Ella Omoto," said Trish.

"Oh, are you from Japan, Ella?" asked Dan.

"Yes. My parents and I moved here last year. My Japanese name is Ayumi but I go by Ella now."

"The food is great," said Dan.

"I'll help myself thank you, Dan," said Trish. "Ella can't eat most of this food, as she can only eat gluten-free foods and I don't see much on the table that she can eat."

"That's ok, Trish," said Ella.

"No it's not," said Dan, "I'll be right back with a gluten-free dessert."

"That's very kind of him, don't you think, Trish?"

"I wonder where he's going to get a gluten-free dessert."

As he said, Dan was back in minutes with a tray of chocolate, fudge brownies for Ella.

"Thank you so much," said Ella as she took the first bite of a brownie. When she took the second bite, she grasped her neck and fell to the floor.

"Ella!" cried Trish.

"Ayumi!" shouted Hiroki who was at her side in seconds.

"Ayumi!" cried Akiko.

"What have you given to my daughter?" yelled Hiroki to Dan standing sheepishly by her side.

Trish called 911 on her cell. The guests circled around Ella's lifeless body.

"What happened?" asked Charlie. "I'll call Dad and have him send Sergeant Frank Brown and Corporal Kurt Lewis. This looks like a crime scene."

Akiko and Hiroki cradled their only child in their arms, wailing, as they listened for her breath but there was none.

Within minutes the EMS arrived and tried to revive her but it looked desperate. They put the body of the fifteen-year-old girl into the EMS ambulance just as Frank and Lewis entered Memorial Hall. They took charge of the crowd, bagged the partially-eaten brownie and arranged for the Omoto's to be in the van with their daughter. Frank and Kurt also listened to Trish who was crying and trying to explain that Gilbert, Dan Redmond, had brought Ella a tray of gluten-free brownies from the catering staff. Dan stood there watching the whole episode evolve right before his eyes.

Frank Brown spoke to Dan first. "What was in those brownies and where did you get them?"

"I...I...I just saw the caterers and they said they had some gluten-free brownies in the kitchen; so they gave me a tray and I gave it to Ella. What just happened? I'm confused."

"We will have to take you into the RCMP station to get your statement," said Lewis patronizingly.

The party was over. The mystery club witnessed a murder at the Confederation Centre. The crowd gradually dispersed but Marilla, the actor from the musical, who wasn't paying attention to the proceedings spied the chocolate treats and picked a brownie off the tray that Dan had placed on the table and began to eat it. Suddenly, Marilla fell to the floor. Immediately Sgt. Brown and Cpl. Lewis were at her side. They called for help as they tried to revive her. Trish and the Camden Mystery Club members were still at Memorial Hall. They witnessed two murders in less than an hour. Lewis and Brown took the half-eaten brownie and the remaining tray of brownies and sealed them in a collection bag. Another EMS vehicle arrived. The crew tried to revive her but it was hopeless. They took her on a stretcher and placed her in the ambulance and took her to the Queen Elizabeth Hospital.

The EMS team pulled into the QEH and the emergency crew lifted out and lowered the body onto a stretcher, the dead body of Ella Omoto. They took her to the morgue with hysterical parents behind them. Dr. Mack Pathius was there.

The second EMS team arrived at the hospital and took the body of the actress, Marilla, into the morgue as well. Mack said, "Two from the same party? This is unbelievable."

CHAPTER 2

Trish was despondent. The mystery club tried to support her in the loss of her good friend, Ella, but she couldn't hear their words of sympathy. Her mind and heart were in severe pain. John Freeman spoke to Trish, "Did you have a premonition about this, Trish?"

That brought her out of her misery as she said, "No, John. I did not. But we will get to the end of this tragedy in some way." Staff Sergeant Rob Camden, arrived at the scene. He wanted to comfort his daughter but also wanted to know what Frank and Kurt found out. He was told by one of the actors that Marilla was played by Evelyn Storey. The detectives were creating a list of suspects. Dan Redmond was at the top of the list as he sat quietly on a chair waiting to be sent to the RCMP headquarters. George Rayner, the head chef in the kitchen said Hiroki had the party catered to by some Japanese chefs and waitresses. The two detectives put George on their list as well, as he was in the kitchen where the gluten-free brownies were found. Then the catering group was considered. They consisted of Genzo Yamamoto, Fuyuki Yoshimurai, Daigo Suzuki, Aki Nakamura, and Maho Sato. Brown and Lewis asked them where the gluten-free brownies were kept. In his broken English Fuyuki said they were on a shelf near the doorway entrance into the kitchen and they had a sign on them saying they were gluten free. The caterers didn't put the gluten-free brownies out unless someone asked specifically for them. The waitresses who kept the table supplied with food, Aki and Maho, just left them on the shelf. Genzo was the head of the caterers and he said, "This has never happened before. This is bad for business. Who would poison these brownies?"

The entire staff of caterers was asked to come down to the station to give their statements. Sgt. Brown and Cpl. Lewis made their way to the police station to collect individual statements from all of their suspects.

Rob stayed with the mystery club. "Well, there is no need for you to stay here. Trish, I'm very sorry for these deaths especially your friend, Ella. Please accept my condolences."

"We will be having a club meeting tomorrow night," she said with rising anger. "We will find the killer if it's the last thing I do in my entire life! First thing is what killed Ella and Evelyn instantly. Dad, your detectives will see to it that Jennifer Gabble and Erica Bradson determine what the heck was in those brownies."

"Charlie, will you drive Trish home? As for the rest of you, Paul, can you drive the twins Josie and John home?"

Charlie and Paul nodded. The actors were upset about Evelyn.

Matthew from the musical bowed down to the other actors and said, "This is not a very good way to end the season of the musical. Evelyn's family must know. I'll go to her home to tell them."

The mystery club was the last to leave the Confederation Centre that night.

At the RCMP station, Frank and Kurt took statements from all the suspects trying to separate the truth from fictitious speculations. The Japanese were difficult to interpret with their broken English. Genzo, George, and Dan spoke good English. The rest were upset and speaking half-English and half- Japanese. It was getting late. Darkness settled around the headquarters. Frank and Kurt completed their initial interviews looking for alibis. The suspects handed in their names, addresses, and phone numbers. It was quite a night. They were released until more data could incriminate them.

The next day the fudge brownies that Frank and Kurt had were delivered to Jennifer and Erica. It didn't take them very long to determine the murder weapon. The poison was the deadly drug fentanyl. The brownies were laced with it, all six of them.

CHAPTER 3

Trish had a restless night. She dozed in and out of sleep replaying the scene from the night before, trying to put mental pieces of Gilbert and Ella together. *Gilbert, what was his name, Dan Redmond, yes that's it... got the fudge brownies from the kitchen where George was head chef. They were on a shelf near the door. Hiroki and Akiko were frantic as they held their daughter... EMS came...took the body away... then another person ate a brownie... was it Marilla... yes...and she too dropped dead... poison.* Trish awoke. It was 3:00 a.m. Her instincts started to fill her mind. She must go to Hiroki and Akiko. She filled her mind with the feelings of their loss. Her heart ached. Was there any connection between the deaths of Ella and Marilla/Evelyn Storey? Prioritizing her plans for the day, Trish began to type up notes on her laptop. She would take John with her to the Omoto's house. Charlie was too detached from the mystery club. John and Josie were still interested. John was the one who asked about her premonitions. He should be there with her. After their meeting with Ella's parents, they should check out Dad's input from Brown and Lewis. At 4:30 a.m. Trish put her laptop down and slept until her alarm went off at 7:00 a.m. She showered and dressed and met up with Charlie in the kitchen. Lately, Charlie showed a lack of interest in the mystery club. He was up to his eyeballs in his course load at UPEI and basketball and hockey kept him busy enough. His relationship with Josie had fizzled out and she whole heartedly supported Trish in the Camden Mystery Club. Charlie at nineteen, was interested in dating someone his own age. Now that Trish had her driver's license, Dad said they'd have to share the old Toyota. Charlie wasn't too happy about that. At breakfast Charlie asked, "How did you sleep after the party last night?"

Trish said, "Ok. I've had better nights." She wasn't going to share the truth about her lack of sleep. "Can I have the car today?"

"I need to get to a basketball game by 2 p.m. but you can have it this morning," he said.

"You sound as if you are in a very agreeable mood for a change. I'll use it this morning. Thanks."

Trish headed to her room to text John. *Can u come with me to c Ella's parents this am?*

Yah.

I'll pick u up at 9. Ok Trish and John had had previous visits with grieving people; so they knew what to expect. Hiroki answered the door. Trish reached out and put her arms around him and they started to cry together. Akiko opened the door wider and Trish noticed her tear-stained face. "Oh, Akiko, I'm so very sorry for your loss and you too, Hiroki," as she let go of Hiroki and hugged Akiko. The tears were fresh and free flowing. John stood awkwardly at the door.

"Please come in," said Hiroki.

Trish introduced John to the Omoto couple and they went into the living room to visit. The Kleenex box was on the coffee table and within reach of all of them. When tears subsided Trish said, "Why? Why did this happen? Why did Ella have to die? Can you help me to understand any of this incomprehensible death?"

Hiroki said in a hushed tone, "Yakuza."

Akiko was disturbed at her husband's answer. She said, "Ssh, Hiroki. We do not say that name here in Canada."

John was tuned in to the beginnings of the conversation and wanted Hiroki to repeat what he said. "What did you say Hiroki, yakoosa?"

Trish was listening too and she wanted to hear more. Hiroki spoke softly as if the walls could hear, "Yakuza, the criminal underworld of Japan. That is why we moved to Prince Edward Island. They were threatening me before we came here."

Akiko shuddered at the thought. Trish and John were all ears. Hiroki went on, "I was a businessman, an investor in all sorts of businesses worldwide. I became quite well off and kept my dealings with businesses on the right side of the law. Yakuza was on the wrong side of the law and I began getting texts from some of their followers. They were jealous and enraged at my success. I had to bring my daughter here where we were not affected by them. They must have found me and had one of their followers murder Ayumi." Akiko cried again. Hiroki wrapped his arms around her. "Hiroki, this is dangerous to talk about them. We can never prove they were behind it all."

Trish said, "Yes we can and we will if you'll allow us to do our work as the Camden Mystery Club. We will work alongside of the detectives at the RCMP headquarters. Just say yes to our involvement."

"It is risky, but I know you've been involved in other cases; so if Akiko agrees and your father agrees we will approve," said Hiroki. Akiko nodded. "What kind of poison did they use to kill her?"

"That will be easy to find out," said John, "they probably know at the station by now."

"Who is the Japanese catering service you hired?" asked Trish.

"I heard of them through an online source and that they were fairly new to the island and were looking for business. I have a brochure about them if you'd like to have it. They mailed it to me a few weeks ago," said Hiroki. Akiko got up and disappeared into the kitchen.

John whispered to Trish, "This brochure might be a very good lead."

"For sure."

Hiroki brought back the pamphlet and passed it to Trish.

Trish and John sat while Akiko arrived back with some tea and they sipped on it while talking about all the wonderful things Ayumi/Ella did in her brief life. John told them about several funeral homes.

When it was time to leave, they hugged and cried and talked about grief. Akiko motioned to Trish to please come by anytime. "Come back, soon," she said.

"We will," said Trish. "So sorry. So very sorry, good- bye."

While Trish drove John home she said, "We have lots of things to discuss at our meeting tonight."

"Are we going to look at the brochure before the meeting?" asked John.

"Of course, silly. Can we have a private room to peruse it at your home? Josie will want to see it if she's home."

"I think she had a class or something this morning but we can check it out in my room."

CHAPTER 4

The Camden Mystery Club was very solemn that night as each spoke kind words of Ella in the basement rec. room of the Camden house. Once that was over, Trish and John began to share their experience of their visit with Ella's parents. The group appeared small as Ella and Charlie weren't there. Josie and John, the Freeman twins and Paul, who was fashionably late with his munchies were the only ones with Trish. "Where is Charlie tonight?" asked Josie. She knew he was probably trying to avoid her. They had a mutual agreement to break up and begin to see other people.

"He said he was going to be at the university tonight," said Trish.

Trish and John filled in the day's news including the hush hush word, 'Yakuza' that Hiroki spoke so fearfully and the brochure. As well Trish had checked with her dad and found out that the poison was fentanyl. The conversation started around the pamphlet. It looked as if it were a copy printed off of Hiroki's printer which he hadn't mentioned to say. It was in color titled, 'New Catering Service in PEI' serving Canadian or Japanese foods for any occasion. There were pictures of a variety of foods and a chef with a tall, white hat smiling on the front. For more information check out our website at www.cateringpei.ca. "John and I checked out the website and there were names of several men and women listed as workers with chef Genzo. He runs the business. Daigo Suzuki and Fuyuki Yoshimurai as well as Aki Nakamura and Maho Sato were also listed and emails for each of them were in the brochure."

"You've come up with a lot of information today," said Paul. "Do you know what Yakuza means? It is the largest Mafia group in the world."

"Here we go again," said Josie remembering the last case they were not allowed to research.

"Does your father know you know about the Yakuza?" asked Paul.

"No, I didn't tell him about our visit to the Omoto's this morning except that they were very upset and experiencing shock and grief."

"Then I would suggest we use the blackboard to list our suspects and leave out the word "Yakuza", said Paul. "Go ahead, Trish and make a list."

Trish began with the most obvious, Gilbert, i.e., Dan Redmond, George Rayner, Genzo Yamamoto, Daigo Suzuki, Fuyuki Yoshimurai, Aki Nakamura, and Maho Sato. They were all there and all had access to the fudge brownies. Any one of them could have poisoned the tray of gluten-free brownies. Dad said detectives Frank Brown and Kurt Lewis had the brownies checked by the forensics girls, Jennifer and Erica and it didn't take very long to find out that the whole tray of six brownies was laced with fentanyl. Trish said, "Maybe Marilla, I mean, Evelyn Storey's act of taking a poisonous brownie was an unlucky coincidence. Dad also said that Dr. Mack Pathius took blood samples from the bodies and the lab concluded it was fentanyl that killed them both."

"If the Yakuza are behind this dual murder they had to have a front man to do the dirty work and they had to have an 'in' with one of our suspects," said Paul.

"How long have these Japanese people been living here in PEI?" asked Josie. "We have to do some research on their lives. Do we have any information on the statements they gave to Sgt. Brown and Cpl. Lewis?"

"Good question, Josie. We haven't followed up with their initial interviews. We could check with Dad about the detective's work tonight after our meeting," said Trish. "Another thing is, both Ella's and Evelyn's funerals will probably be the day after tomorrow; so I think we should confirm the time and place of the funerals and our club should attend both, if possible."

"I'll call the Fulton and Davison Funeral Homes in the morning. These are the likely funeral homes in the Charlottetown area and I'll find out times and places for both funerals," said John.

"Tomorrow's plan then is to follow up on the catering service suspects, find out about the funerals, and keep us all in the loop by text," said Trish. "If it's ok with you, Josie and Paul, I'd like to take John back to Hiroki and Akiko's to offer any help with funeral preparations."

"That's fine with me," said John.

Paul and Josie nodded their approval. The mystery club ended their meeting and said their good-byes.

Trish didn't want to apply too much pressure on her dad as he was relaxing reading a newspaper in the living room. It was half past nine. "Anything interesting in the news?" she asked as she broke the silence.

"There is an article about the two deaths at the Confederation Centre last night."

"Can I read it?" "Here."

Trish read a brief piece that the RCMP was looking into the suspicious deaths of a girl and a woman at the Confederation Centre. No names were given.

She passed the paper back to dad. "Did Sgt. Brown and Cpl. Lewis find any information from the statements they took last night?"

"I know you want to take this mystery on as a case and I will help you whenever I can but the truth is there are too many suspects and it's too early to tell which ones are telling the truth. Frank and Kurt had problems communicating with several of the Japanese, as their English wasn't that great."

Trish didn't mention the brochure that Hiroki had given her. She decided to keep it for future mystery club use. "I'm going to head off to bed. I'll see you in the morning. Good night."

"Night."

CHAPTER 5

John was true to his word. He called the funeral homes in the morning and found out that Ella's funeral was at the Fulton Funeral Home at 10:30 a.m. the next day and that Evelyn's funeral was at the Davison Funeral Home on that same day at 2:00 p.m. He sent a text to Trish and she texted him back. They were planning to meet at Hiroki's house at ten.

When they arrived, an unknown car was in the driveway. They rang the bell. Hiroki answered it. "Oh, hello, Trish and John. We have the funeral director here right now helping us with funeral plans. Can you come back in an hour?"

"Sure," said Trish. "We'll be back. See you."

"John, do you want to go to Tim's for a coffee to put in time while we wait?" asked Trish.

"Yah, ok."

They walked to Tim's in Cornwall and ordered coffees. They sat down and Trish took a note pad out of her purse with the catering brochure. She took the pamphlet and studied it. Sometimes she'd get a premonition about people. She wasn't having much luck today.

The silence between them broke when John said, "Would you like to go to a movie with me sometime Trish?"

"Really, John? Sure if you want to, I'll go with you.

What kind of movies do you like?"

"I like most movies but I really like action films and mystery movies."

"Well, let me know when a good one comes along and we can ask Paul and Josie if they want to come as well."

Things were not going as planned. John had just gotten enough courage to ask Trish out on a date and here she thinks it's a club activity. John said, "I was hoping just you and I could see a movie together. We could go out for Chinese food afterwards."

Trish didn't want to hurt John's feelings as she had practically grown up with John and Josie since her mom died. The Freeman's were close friends of her dad and they spent many shared barbeques at each other's houses. "John, are you asking me out on a date?"

"Yah, I am."

"Ok. Have you got a movie in mind?"

"There is one coming out at the Cineplex called, "Mystery at Lawrence Point. I thought it might be interesting."

"Ok. Just you and I will go, but remember we've been friends for a long time and I only see you in that way, John."

"That's fine."

"I've been studying this brochure but I'm not getting any vibes or premonitions from it," said Trish.

"It's about time we headed back to the Omoto's, anyway," said John.

They were getting their exercise today as they walked the fifteen minutes back to Hiroki and Akiko's place. The car was gone. Hiroki answered the door. "Come in," he said.

"How are you today?" asked Trish.

"We are coping, but it is very painful," said Hiroki. "Not much sleep."

"Your funeral plans are with the Fulton Funeral Home. Tomorrow at 10:30?"

"Yes, I will speak about my daughter. I've been told it is called a eulogy. The chapel at the funeral home is where it is to take place and there will be a small reception afterwards."

"Do you want any help with the funeral?" asked Trish.

"No, thank you. You will come?" asked Hiroki. "Most definitely." said Trish. "The whole mystery club will be there. We won't stay for tea today. We just wanted to check that you have all your plans in order. We'll see ourselves out. See you tomorrow morning. Bye."

Trish and John left and headed over to Trish's house. Charlie was getting ready to leave for the university when they arrived. "Can I drive you into UPEI, so John and I can have the car today?"

"I'm ready to go. I have a class at noon. I will let you have the car if you'll pick me up after classes."

"It's a deal," said Trish.

The three got into the car and off they went to the university to drop off Charlie. Trish told Charlie about the funeral plans for Ella and he said he'd try to make it. Trish and John had other plans for the day. They were going to the RCMP headquarters.

Sgt. Brown and Cpl. Lewis were perusing the information they got from the statements. They weren't expecting Trish and John at the office but respected their involvement as Trish's dad was their boss.

"Can we share some information?" asked Trish as John and she approached the office of Sgt. Brown.

"We don't have much to share but you may come in if you like. Hello John, how is your father enjoying retirement?"

"He's doing fine."

"You should ask him to drop in for a visit someday," said Frank. "I suppose you want to discuss our suspects."

"Yes, if you've got a moment," said Trish.

Frank began by telling them that Genzo started up his catering business a year ago and hired his staff at that time. The two young men, Fuyuki and Daigo, both had catering experience in Japan and were hired on first. The girls, Aki and Maho, were also hired on shortly after. The four of them spoke Japanese fluently and were learning the English language at work through Genzo who spoke only English to them. The business worked like this: they would take orders online from their website and would fill them according to the preferred foods that were suggested by the client. Hiroki ordered Canadian foods, sandwiches and sweets for the party. He did not think of gluten-free options until Genzo suggested that it was a good idea to have a sample of gluten-free dessert in case someone at the party had that food requirement. Hiroki agreed and Genzo made the fudge brownies himself. He said he did not put poison in the brownies.

We interrogated Dan Redmond but all he said was he just grabbed the brownies off the shelf where the sign said gluten free. He had no idea they were laced with poison. Then there was George who owns the restaurant and is in and out of the kitchen and supported the Japanese catering service by allowing the staff to store their food in the kitchen while looking after the restaurant. He said he was the one to put the brownies on the shelf by the door and he made a gluten-free sign for Genzo. As far as the rest of the suspects go, we had a very hard time understanding their broken English but they all said, "No poison." Aki and Maho were the waitresses and would refill plates when they were empty. Fuyuki and Daigo prepared the sandwiches and sweets at their kitchen in the Confederation Mall and transferred them through the underground tunnel to Memorial Hall during the performance of the musical.

Frank paused waiting for the two young detectives to come up with questions or share the information that they had. Trish spoke, "Genzo made the brownies himself. What would be his motive to poison Ella?"

"He started up the business himself and wouldn't want to jeopardize anything to cause his catering service to go under," said Lewis.

"It would be easy for someone to inject the poison into the already-made brownies in the kitchen at the Mall before transporting them to the restaurant at the Confederation Centre," said Trish. "How can we communicate with the Japanese caterers?"

"Genzo speaks both Japanese and English. He could be a translator," said John.

"What do you have to share with us?" asked Frank.

"We have the brochure Hiroki had when placing the food order," said Trish as she showed it to the detectives. "It includes not only a website for Genzo to receive orders but it also has email addresses for the staff that work for him."

"That doesn't help with the language barrier. The four workers for Genzo need a translator as John suggested," said Frank, "I think we need to find our own translator, so Genzo doesn't lie to us during a translating session. He is still a very strong suspect."

Trish and John left the headquarters and texted the other club members to be at the funeral homes the next day. They were going to look for a Japanese-English translator.

CHAPTER 6

The Camden Mystery Club was the first to arrive at the Fulton Funeral Home. They seated themselves on the left-hand side near the front of the chapel. Sgt. Brown and Cpl. Lewis arrived and seated themselves behind the mystery club. Hiroki and Akiko slid into the front row just before Charlie landed and seated himself with the club members. The funeral director was at the back of the chapel and the chaplain came in from a side door. The service was about to begin when Trish started to have a tingling sense of someone coming into the chapel and sitting at the back on the right-hand side. From her viewpoint she turned inconspicuously to see a person wearing a hoodie covering their identity and seated at the back. She had a premonition that this person was the killer. She couldn't check this person out; so she sat through the brief service and Hiroki's eulogy which was emotional and endearing. As soon as the eulogy was over, the figure disappeared. When the service was over, the congregation went into the reception room. Trish thought of the figure at the back. He was of an average build but was well disguised. She asked the funeral director if he saw anything when the person arrived. He said he was late and looked as if he didn't want to be recognized. "He left just after Hiroki's eulogy", the funeral director mentioned. Trish was troubled. *Why would the killer check out the funeral unless to see for himself the pain Hiroki was experiencing. Could he understand the service? Was the person a he or a she?*

The mystery club listened to Trish describe her sixth sense which always came true. Paul said, "Maybe the killer could understand more English than Sgt. Brown and Cpl. Lewis thought or gave credit towards them."

"Maybe we should find out for ourselves the level of English language the four Japanese caterers actually have," said Trish.

"Well, it's time for lunch," said Paul. "It's a very small number of people here. Do you think there are people here that we should meet?"

Trish looked around the room. There were a couple of neighbors she recognized. Just as she was about to take Paul up on his suggestion she noticed one of the waitresses from the night at Memorial Hall. "Paul, you can go but I'm going to speak to that Japanese woman that was at the Confederation Centre the other night."

Trish walked over to the woman and introduced herself. The woman's name was Aki. John joined in and they began to converse about the night of the deaths. Aki said, "I saw the food was on the table. I served the guests. I didn't know of any poison.

I speak a little English. Genzo is helping me speak English. He is a good boss. I respect him."

"Do you know of any of the members of your catering service who use drugs or can get drugs for poison?" asked Trish.

Aki looked frightened. She said, "I do not know. No poison. No drugs."

Trish noticed her change in manner. She persisted, "Aki, I think you know something you are not telling me. Who can get drugs and how can the poison be put in the brownies?"

"I must go. I do not know of these bad things."

CHAPTER 7

Paul had his lunch, a cheeseburger and fries from Burger King. The other club members had bagged lunches from home. They didn't have much time to discuss the events at the Ella funeral before turning up at the Evelyn Storey funeral which was held at the Saint Andrew's Church because the Davison Funeral Home was too small for such a large crowd. They went in as a group and sat near the back. Lewis and Brown were there. Many people showed up; the entire cast of the summer shows, the orchestra, Dan Redmond, and George Rayner. Other islanders that knew of the Marilla role Evelyn played also came. Alan Derrick, the man who played Matthew in the musical, gave the eulogy. He said Evelyn was like a true sister to him and that they were very good friends.

Charlie wasn't able to make the funeral for Ms. Storey but he did let the club know that he was sorry. The reception was catered to by the women's church group. Trish, Josie, John, and Paul circulated through the crowd talking to familiar faces. Trish and John also talked to the detectives. Trish spied Dan Redmond speaking to Evelyn's husband. When Dan moved away, Trish made a beeline towards him. "Dan, I'm so sorry for your loss. Can you explain how Evelyn didn't know that Ella was on the floor at Memorial Hall and you put the tray on the table where Evelyn could take a brownie and eat it?" Trish was her bold and brazen self.

"It was an accident. Evelyn talked to several people who crowded around her after the show and didn't notice me placing the tray on the table. It was my fault that the tray was on the table. I will always be sorry for that. It was an unfortunate coincidence. I did not kill Ella, or Evelyn on purpose. I did not add poison to the gluten-free brownies. I didn't even know Ella."

Trish moved on and overheard Frank talking to the restaurant owner. She listened. Frank was discussing the crime scene with George Rayner. "Can you please assist me in understanding how the brownies were injected with poison before or after they came from the kitchen in the Confederation Mall?"

"I have no idea. I put them on the shelf by the door and I made a sign 'Gluten Free'. That's all," said George.

"Who knew that Ella could eat only gluten-free foods?" asked Frank.

"That is the million-dollar question. Who knew this would somehow lead to the killer," said George.

"You are still a suspect in this investigation. Who told you that the brownies were gluten-free?"

"Genzo brought them into the kitchen and said they were to be kept separate from the other foods. He said they were gluten-free; so I put them on the shelf and made the sign so the waitresses wouldn't get them mixed up with the other foods. You will excuse me. I have nothing more to say." George left Frank and met up with some of the actors who talked about how wonderful Evelyn was.

Trish searched the room for the club members to tell them about the conversation she just overheard. She saw Paul at the food table; so she made her way to him. "Have you seen John and Josie?" she asked.

"They were talking to Dan Redmond a few minutes ago. Do you have some information to share?" Paul asked.

"Oh, there they are. Come Paul, I have something to discuss with you guys." Trish took Paul by the arm and they made their way through the crowd to the twins.

"Any news?" asked John.

"I heard a conversation between Sgt. Brown and George Rayner. Brown asked George who knew that Ella could eat only gluten-free foods? I knew that because we were good friends. Did you guys know that?" asked Trish.

They all nodded. They knew that she could eat only gluten-free foods.

"We know that Genzo made a sampling of gluten- free foods for the party. How did he know she was gluten-free?"

"Maybe he didn't know. Maybe he just wanted to have something to serve to guests who couldn't eat things made with flour," said Paul.

"I think we have to keep him under surveillance," said Josie.

"I agree," said John.

"This morning I talked to Aki at Ella's funeral. She looked scared when I mentioned drugs and poison," said Trish. "I think we should check out the other catering staff. Do you agree? I know the killer was at Ella's funeral. I just know it."

The three mystery club members all agreed to meet up with Trish that evening at the club house in the basement of the Camden residence. The guests at the reception started to filter out so the club said they'd see each other a few hours from now back in Cornwall.

CHAPTER 8

They started their meeting with chatter about the funerals of the day. Hiroki's eulogy was very different from the one Alan Derrick gave. The small attendance at Ella's funeral and the large gathering at Evelyn's funeral didn't compare. They looked at the blackboard to see what they already covered and where they were to go from there. They all noticed that they hadn't checked out the three other Japanese caterers on the board. "Let's find out how much English Genzo's staff actually understand," said Trish, "I believe they have more intelligence than we have given them credit for. Let's go back to the kitchen in the Confederation Mall and find out who made all the food. We can interview them individually. There is Daigo, Fuyuki, and Maho we haven't spoken to yet." The club agreed.

Trish and John were voted to go to the kitchen in the Mall. The next items on the roster were some very important questions that they all shared.

Paul asked, "How does the killer obtain fentanyl? What does he do? Inject the poison into the brownies?"

"How can he do this without being noticed by the other caterers?" asked Josie.

"Do they all know about the poison or is it just one, two, or three of them?" asked Trish. "It looks as if we've got our work cut out for us. John and I will text you tomorrow when we find out more from our Japanese cooks. Meeting is adjourned."

The friends socialized for an hour; then headed for home. Trish said she'd have the use of the car in the morning and she'd pick up John at nine.

"Trish, do you know where this kitchen is in the Confederation Mall?" asked John.

"I think it's on the lower level."

Trish parked the car and the two young detectives left the vehicle and entered the mall heading for the kitchen. They went down the steps and looked around; no kitchen. "I was sure it was in the basement. Maybe it's on the upper level where the other restaurants are located." They traipsed upstairs and continued their search. "They've moved!"

"But where?" asked John.

"I don't know but my sixth sense tells me we're too late. We've missed them."

"Think, Trish. Where would they go and are there any remains of their work done here before they relocated."

"My first hunch was the lower level. Let's go back there and take a thorough examination of the area."

This time Trish's intuition was predominant. They noticed a boarded-up, sealed-off space that might have been the section where the food was produced. The doorway was locked but Trish had broken locks before; so she tried a fingernail file, then a key, then a wire she kept in her purse. The wire worked. The door opened. They entered to find ample equipment that indicated the room was used as a production of food for distribution. There was an oven, flour on the table, left-over serving plates and Trish's favorite, a waste basket full of rubbish. Trish was used to searching for clues in garbage cans. She knew if she found anything significant she couldn't use her bare hands to touch the items, as it could be evidence and she would leave fingerprints on it. She dumped the trash on the floor. She spread it out with her feet. There was a lot of wax paper, paper towel, left-over crusts of bread, and a syringe. "The jackpot!" she cried.

"Way to go, Trish," said John.

She used some paper towel to collect the needle and wrapped it in some wax paper. "We'll have to take it down to the RCMP headquarters," said Trish. "Let's go!" She stashed it in her purse and they were off.

Excitedly they left for the station. They met up with Cpl. Lewis in the reception area. "Cpl. Lewis, we have found some evidence we think you may find very helpful," Trish said respectfully.

"Come into my office and tell me what you've found."

Trish pulled out the wax paper and passed it to Kurt. He took it and gradually pulled away the paper to expose the syringe. "Where did you find this?"

"We believe that the caterers used a space in the Confederation Mall to make the food for the party. When we went there, the place was closed and boarded up." She didn't say she picked the lock. "We went in to find evidence that they had used the room and I checked the garbage can and found this needle. We believe it has something to do with the fentanyl used in poisoning the brownies."

"Thank you, John and Trish. I'll take it to the forensics team to have it analyzed."

"What are your plans for your investigation, today?" he asked.

"Well," Trish said hesitantly, "we were hoping to meet up with the Japanese caterers, wherever they may be."

"I may be able to help you in your search," said Lewis. "I spoke with Aki at Ella Omoto's funeral. I have an address for her. Check it out. I don't know if it will be of any help for you but it might lead to something else."

"Thank you," said John and Trish simultaneously. "Gee, Cpl. Lewis is being uncharacteristically very helpful," John said to Trish as they left.

CHAPTER 9

Jennifer and Erica found traces of fentanyl in the syringe. It was solid evidence. They also found a good fingerprint on the needle. Some more evidence.

Trish typed the address Cpl. Lewis gave them into the GPS. The two teenage detectives were confident that this would uncover some of the mystery of Ella's death. When they arrived at the address, they were in front of a duplex in downtown Charlottetown. They rang the doorbell. No answer, but there was the muffled sound of someone moving about; so they tried it again. Aki came to the door. "May we have a word with you, Aki?" asked Trish.

"No drugs. No Poison."

"We just want to talk to you," John said.

"Where are the other caterers living?" asked Trish.

"I don't know English. Go away."

"I heard a noise as if there was someone else in your duplex. Do you have company?" asked Trish.

Fearfully Aki said it was Daigo. They lived together. "Can we come in and talk about the party?" asked John.

"Wait." She closed the door and went into the kitchen. In a moment she was back. "You can come in, says Daigo."

Trish and John were escorted into the living space of the tiny duplex. Aki motioned for them to sit down on the couch. Daigo appeared from the kitchen. Aki and Daigo sat on a large orange, bean bag chair.

Trish wanted some answers. She couldn't help herself from being forthright. "Who had the poison and where did they get it?"

Daigo spoke. "We don't do drugs. We are afraid of the system here and we are worried about the others working for Genzo. They are not like us. We share this house because our money isn't very much and we help each other pay the rent."

"Why did the kitchen in the mall disappear and where is Genzo setting up business now?" asked Trish.

"Genzo was afraid for business. He told us to stay home today and he would text us when he had a new location for business," said Daigo.

"What did you mean when you said you were not like the others? How can we find them?" asked John.

"Fuyuki and Maho are out of town. They live in Stratford. They are not helpful and will not assist you. They are a couple. Aki and I are friends. We share our living space to save us money. That is all," said Daigo.

"Could you please give us their address?" asked Trish.

"I am afraid for you. They will know that I gave you their address and it may be difficult for us to work together if you see them at their home. I will not give you their address. I have said too much already. When Genzo contacts us, I will give you our new business address by text. That is as much as I can do," said Daigo.

"Thank you, Daigo. You've been a great help. Don't worry about us. We have been solving mysteries for a very long time," said Trish. Trish and John said their good-byes and texted the mystery club members from the car.

When Frank Brown heard about Kurt Lewis giving Aki's address to Trish and John, he was furious, "Why you bumbling idiot, we haven't even contacted her since the night of the party and here you are giving away a lead for the Camden Mystery Club. They will have visited her already. Now we have to play 'catch up' with Trish and her club. That's not how things are supposed to work around here. We take the lead and the CMC can follow.

Got it? And another thing, Trish and John Freeman found a syringe at the mall kitchen site and gave it to you? You did give it to Jennifer and Erica didn't you?"

"Yes I did and they've found fentanyl in the syringe. If you didn't have your other priorities all mixed up, you would have known that Jennifer and Erica found the evidence in the needle," retaliated Lewis.

"Well, we had better get over to Aki's place immediately," said Frank anxiously as he knew he hadn't been in touch with the case as thoroughly as he should have been.

Frank and Lewis arrived at the address that Lewis had given to Trish. Frank sounded formal and Lewis sounded casual in their conversation with Aki and Daigo. They were given the same answers the two had given to Trish and John. They were also given the same warnings about Fuyuki and Maho as well as the information about Genzo setting up a new workspace.

The detectives left. Frank realized the night of the party the Japanese caterers' English was hard to understand but today they were fairly easy to comprehend. He justified this thought with the fact that the caterers were in an extremely tense situation at the party and now in their own home were much calmer and able to express their thoughts in English.

"Let's go over to see Hiroki again," said Trish to John as they drove away from Aki and Daigo's duplex. "I think we have to listen to some of his story about coming to PEI and leaving Japan."

"That's a good idea, Trish. By the way, that mystery movie is on at the Cineplex. Would you like to go tonight?"

"Sure," said Trish.

They arrived back in Cornwall. Hiroki and Akiko were all alone. Trish rang the doorbell and Hiroki answered it.

"Welcome. Come in. Akiko and I are very tired of our painful thoughts and it is good of you to come and lift our spirits."

They sat in the living room with emotions at the surface of their conversation. Trish began to ask questions about Hiroki's life in Japan. "Yakuza, you said was the largest Japanese underworld organization in the world. Can you refresh my memory about them and the kinds of threats they sent to you, Hiroki?"

"At first, they demanded payment of money from me. I didn't pay. Then the warnings became more urgent when they began to say they'd kill my family if I didn't pay them. That is when Akiko and I decided to leave Japan for good. We were afraid for Ayumi's life and our own."

"How did the Yakuza know that Ella was gluten- free?" asked John.

"They know everything about everyone they target for payments. They could have had her under surveillance through one of their drug dealers or placed a bug in our home. This can happen in Japan easily enough. We made the move but it was too late. The Yakuza had already made a plan to have my daughter murdered no matter where she lived."

Trish was pondering Hiroki's words. "We have the brochure you gave us. How can we find the couple Fuyuki and Maho? We've already spoken to Aki and Daigo. Genzo closed the kitchen in the mall and is going to relocate to another site."

"We found the poison in a needle in the wastepaper basket in the place where they made the food for the party. It has been analyzed and shows the drug fentanyl in the syringe. Do you know about this drug?" asked John.

"Yes, I have heard about its use," said Hiroki.

"You mentioned Fuyuki, Trish. I once dealt with a Fuyuki several years ago. He was an online client of mine. He made an online business deal which wasn't very profitable and he lost his investments. I apologized to him and never heard from him again. Fuyuki is a common Japanese name. Maybe it is the same Fuyuki I don't know but he could have held a grudge about me if it's the same person. In fact, he may be working directly for the Yakuza. Now that would be a real investigation."

Trish was getting that tingling sensation all through her body. Her premonition and intuitive nature were motivated. She said, "We only have his email address on the brochure you gave us. This doesn't sound very helpful. How can we meet this guy in person?"

John said, "Let's do a Google search. The pamphlet gives his full name, Fuyuki Yoshimurai."

CHAPTER 10

Maho Sato was a drug addict. She depended on Fuyuki Yoshimurai to supply drugs for her. She was depressed in her present state in Tokyo living with Fuyuki, being helpless and cut off from her family. Fuyuki told her she couldn't have family ties while he was working for the Yakuza. It was a stipulation of the organization. What she couldn't figure out was their future together. Fuyuki told her he loved her, yet he kept her helpless and supported by him. She was tired of this existence, wanting more, wanting a better life for herself.

Fuyuki wasn't happy either. He was afraid of the Yakuza. He was required to do exactly what he was told to do. The hierarchy of the Yakuza kept him in his low life selling drugs on the street, beating up those who couldn't pay the money they owed, and reporting directly to the next one up the ladder. He wanted to be free of this life. Maho and he wanted to escape from Tokyo, move away, become law-abiding citizens, but the Yakuza would find him wherever they went and they would have him killed. He had been with the organization for ten years, ever since he was sixteen. He knew no other life. Picking up heroin, cocaine, and fentanyl in undisclosed areas of the mammoth city of Tokyo and selling them to a file of users was his life.

He met Maho while working the streets and listened to her story of an unhappy childhood, suffering from a dominant father who controlled her every move and a submissive mother who took the abuse as normal. Fuyuki had a protective feeling for Maho when he met her on the streets in his district in Tokyo. She was making money selling her body to pay for drugs. She liked her dealer, Fuyuki. They used to spend time talking about their youthfulness, loneliness, pain and hopes for the future. Neither could see their way out of Tokyo. It would cost a lot of money to escape and Fuyuki couldn't just walk away from the Yakuza.

Then one day, the two of them noticed an advertisement for a new catering business in Prince Edward Island, Canada. They both began to dream of this adventure and getaway. Maho began to wean herself off of heroin with Fuyuki's help. Fuyuki continued to work for the Yakuza but now he had a plan to breakout. He fearfully requested to meet with the top level of the Yakuza to discuss his future. "If you leave Tokyo, we will find you. If you follow our instructions in your new environment, then we may be able to allow you to start up business in your new location," said the head of the Yakuza. "We have a worldwide connection with our Mafia organization."

Fuyuki left the meeting feeling he couldn't go anywhere without being noticed but when he spoke to Maho she helped him realize that being in a smaller town would in itself help them. Besides, the ad they read was explicit in wanting waitresses and caterers in PEI. They decided to meet with the organizer of the advertisement, Genzo Yamamoto.

Genzo was a law-abiding citizen in Tokyo or so they thought. He was eager to start up a business in PEI, Canada and needed four workers from Japan to follow him to this new territory. Firstly, he said they would have to appreciate some basic knowledge of Japanese and Canadian foods that were easy to prepare. Also they would have to be eager to learn the business world of catering. He already had two Japanese people interested and if Fuyuki and Maho came on board then he'd have his four employees. Genzo was paying the airfare and would start compensating them with a minimum wage when they arrived in PEI. The startup date for the catering business would be in two months. They would need passports. Genzo would be in touch with them on their cell phones in a couple of days to let them know if they would be hired.

Maho and Fuyuki were cautious and relieved when they got the call from Genzo that they were approved for the jobs. Maho knew that the move wouldn't be easy. Fuyuki knew it was not only the beginning of a new life but also the startup of the Yakuza in PEI.

CHAPTER 11

Trish and John did their Google search at the university library on Fuyuki Yoshimurai in Japan and found many Japanese with the very same name. "How can we find out if the Fuyuki who Hiroki named is the one working for Genzo's catering service?" asked Trish.

"We don't have that information," said John who sounded as disappointed as Trish.

"Do you think we could find out where they live?" "That's not possible, Trish. We have no address for them."

"We could get them out of hiding if we sent Fuyuki an email. It could say that we know who they are and that we saw them at the party after the musical the other night and we want to talk to them," said Trish.

"If they are involved in the murders, why would they want to meet with you?"

"You are right. We are in a dilemma. Maybe when Genzo sets up his new kitchen we will be able to interview them. For now we just have to wait. So we may as well head back to Cornwall."

"Well, since we are going to the movie tonight let's head to Boston Pizza for supper, my treat," said John.

"I'm getting hungry. It's almost five. That's a good idea. We can skip Chinese food after the movie, John. Let's go now."

Trish drove the old Toyota from the university to Boston Pizza. They were silent in the car as they were thinking about the case. Trish was thinking about this so-called date with John. She didn't have any feelings for him other than they cared for each other as friends. "So have you heard about this movie, John?"

"I saw the trailer on the computer. It looks like an exceptional mystery."

They were seated at the restaurant and placed their order, a pizza with the works.

Trish had a sleepless night again. She dreamt about Genzo making poisonous brownies and the crowd of people at the Confederation Centre hovering over Ella's body. She awoke feeling emotionally drained. *Genzo made the brownies. Did he add the fentanyl?* She lay awake pondering the situation. If Genzo said it was bad for business, why would he poison the brownies? It just didn't make sense. So did Fuyuki add the fentanyl to the brownies? As if she were in the mystery movie she and John went to last night where everything happened in sequence, she got a text from Daigo. It said, *"Genzo new location Sea Fare kitchen, Stratford. New job starts today.*

Sgt. Frank Brown got the text as well. He noticed on the text that it had gone to Trish Camden and him. Now he had to get things in order to visit the kitchen in Stratford with Trish doing the same. He did not like this one little bit. It was bad enough to take Kurt Lewis with him on his important interrogations but now with Trish and probably John Freeman on the same wavelength it was going to be very difficult. He hoped he would get a head start. Frank looked for Lewis and found him in the forensics lab goofing off with the annoyed girls. Jennifer and Erica were used to his antics but were relieved when Frank came along and dragged Lewis away from their busy schedule.

"We've got to go now," Frank said to Kurt. "What's your hurry," said Kurt.

"I got a text from Daigo. He says they've got a new kitchen in Stratford. He sent the text to Trish Camden and I don't want to let her arrive on the scene before we get there. Got it?"

"Okay. I'm ready. Let's go," said Lewis sarcastically. "You don't have to sound so flippant."

"Sorry."

It was like an amazing race; the two pulled out of the parking lot and headed for Stratford. At the same time, Trish was asking her brother if she could have the car. When he said she could, she sent a text to John and he responded he'd be ready when she got there. They were behind Brown and Lewis as they were leaving from Cornwall and the detectives were already in Charlottetown which gave them a fifteen-minute advantage. Stratford was east of Charlottetown and Cornwall was west of the city. It was 10 a.m. when Frank and Kurt arrived at the Sea Fare Kitchen. They parked the car and made their way to the building. Genzo and his crew were there. The instructions were given by Genzo to the workers in English. He said they were to prepare Japanese food for a local Rotary function that evening. The menu consisted of sushi as appetizer, basmati rice with curry chicken stir fry as entrée as well as a vegetarian stir fry, and parfait and furutsu sando as dessert. Genzo was interrupted by Frank and Kurt.

"Good morning," said Sgt. Brown. "We hope we haven't disturbed your plans for the day. Cpl. Lewis and I have some very important questions to ask you about the poison in the brownies that killed two innocent people last week."

"I am not guilty," said Genzo. "We must prepare enough food to feed fifty persons tonight and we must purchase our required foods this morning."

"I believe you are not guilty but someone in this room is guilty and I intend to find out who the guilty party is," said Frank.

At that moment Trish and John arrived and agreed with Sgt. Brown that Genzo was innocent but they also agreed that someone in that room was guilty as well.

Four detectives, two adult ones and two school-age ones were standing there watching for any uneasiness in the group. The tension was horrific. Minutes lapsed when finally Trish said, "John and I want to interview Fuyuki in private. Is that okay with you Sgt. Brown and Cpl. Lewis?"

"Actually no that is not okay with us, Trish, as we want to have a conversation with him first," said Frank.

"Would it be possible for us to sit in on your dialogue, Sgt. Brown? Dad always says we are good detectives and we can help the RCMP detectives when possible."

Sgt. Brown was in a hard spot. Trish would reveal to her father that they were not cooperative and then they would be reprimanded at the office.

"Very well, Trish. On one condition, that is, you and I consult with Fuyuki alone and leave the other suspects with Cpl. Lewis and John."

The decision was approved and Trish and Frank removed Fuyuki from the kitchen part of the room and went over to an office area. Sgt. Brown knew this was not protocol; however, he wanted to keep in the good books with Trish's father and he also wanted Lewis to question the three other cooks with John.

CHAPTER 12

Fuyuki showed no guilt. He was trained by the Yakuza to become stone-faced when being interrogated by police. Frank questioned him about the fentanyl that was in the syringe found by Trish at the last kitchen at the Confederation Mall. He kept his mouth shut. Trish also tried to get him to break down from his mask of silence. The two of them tried every angle until Trish remembered that Maho was his woman. Then she began,

"Maho and you are a couple, am I right?" No response.

"Maho needs you and you don't provide for her the things she needs. The Yakuza have kept you in their sight for a long time. Maho may be in danger if you don't protect her."

Frank picked up on Trish's line of thought. "You'll never see Maho from prison. You'd better talk or I'll bring Maho in here right now and threaten her with physical pain."

"If you won't talk, we have ways of making you talk," said Trish.

Frank went to the door and called for Maho to come into the office. Lewis and John had been conversing with the three back in the kitchen but with no signs of confession from any of them. Maho and Fuyuki stood in the office now with Trish and Frank.

"Maho," said Frank, "tell us about your relationship with Fuyuki. Is he your dealer, your lover, or are you prepared to let him go to jail? Please have a seat while you think about what I just said."

Maho looked at Fuyuki. He looked different. He looked like an empty shell of a human being. She became frightened. *What should she say? Should she spill the beans about their life in Japan? How she had worked so hard at becoming clean before they were hired by Genzo? Should she tell of the Yakuza? Would Fuyuki still love her if she broke the silence?*

"You are only prolonging the inevitable which means you must talk here or we'll take you for a ride to the RCMP station," said Frank. With that he pushed her chair and tilted it backwards.

Maho spoke. "No pain, will talk." Frank put the chair in an upright position while Maho began. "Fuyuki and I met in Tokyo five years ago. He looked after my needs."

"What kind of needs?" asked Trish.

"He provided me with a room, food, and clothing. I was abandoned by my family. I became a street girl selling my body for drug money. Fuyuki helped me by supplying the drugs I needed. He took care of me and I was dependent on him."

"You said Fuyuki supplied you with drugs. Is he still your dealer?" asked Frank.

"No. I am clean for the first time in my life. Fuyuki wanted to leave the Yakuza behind in Japan but they came with us."

"What do you mean by that?" asked Trish.

"The Yakuza are everywhere. You don't have to look very far to see the damage they have done in people's lives."

"In North America we call the Yakuza the Mafia. Do you know about the deadly drug fentanyl? It was used to kill my friend, Ella."

"Did Fuyuki use the drug to inject it into the gluten- free brownies at the Confederation Centre?"

"Fuyuki doesn't tell me everything. I don't know of his plan to use fentanyl. I don't see him killing people. I only know he is kind and good to me."

Fuyuki just stood in silence. Frank said, "Fuyuki you have access to the drug scene here in PEI. I will have to take you in to the headquarters for further interrogation. Maho, please escort Fuyuki and me to the police car outside."

Frank took Maho by the arm. Trish went back to John and Lewis took hold of Fuyuki's arm and was about to lead him back to the RCMP vehicle when he broke loose and began to run as fast as he could out of the building and across the street. Frank and Lewis began the chase, darting across several lines of traffic past the Tim's and past Stratford Town Hall. Fuyuki was faster and Frank and Lewis were lagging behind. Fuyuki went down a hill and into a wooded area. The detectives didn't see where he went.

"Damn," said Lewis, "he got away."

"We'd better check on Trish to see if we still have Maho in custody," said Frank.

Trish had Maho, Aki, and Daigo back at the kitchen. Genzo had left to pick up groceries for the evening dinner. When he returned and found out that Fuyuki had fled he was only concerned with the food preparations for the Rotary Club dinner.

The detectives and mystery club detectives were in agreement to take Maho into custody in the hope that Fuyuki would try to rescue her and let the other two caterers work at the kitchen. Genzo was beside himself, as he had no one to replace the two Japanese cooks. Trish said, "Genzo, John and I will help you prepare the meal. Just tell us what you want us to do."

Genzo grumbled but knew he needed the help. "I will not pay you. This is volunteer work for you."

"That's okay. We don't mind, do we, John?" "It's okay," said John.

Frank and Kurt took Maho to the department and placed her in an interrogation room.

Kurt Lewis who hadn't been in the office back at the Sea Fare kitchen building wanted an update on Brown's collected information. Brown filled him in on the relationship between Maho and Fuyuki.

"She must know about his drug dealings in Japan and how he gets the drugs in Prince Edward Island," said Lewis. "She has to know. She'd be an idiot to not know his dealings here."

"The Yakuza have Fuyuki well-trained. He escaped from us now but he will want to rescue Maho from us at some point. The thing is, how long are we able to keep her on suspicion of aiding Fuyuki and not having enough evidence to charge him?" asked Frank.

"I should go in and interview her," said Lewis.

"That's not a good idea right now. Give her time to recover from the experience Trish and I just had. I left her cell phone with her. Maybe she'll text Fuyuki."

"Do we have the recorder turned on and do we have someone who can translate for us from Japanese into English?" asked Lewis.

"Of course, Kurt," said Frank, "I always check for these things."

"We can watch her from this two-way mirror to see if she is trying to connect with Fuyuki."

"Who can translate for us?" asked Lewis.

"Why, Hiroki Omoto will come at the drop of a hat. I will contact him and I know he will come as he, too, wants to find the killer of his daughter."

CHAPTER 13

Staff Sergeant Rob Camden was on the phone when Frank and Lewis brought Maho to the RCMP Headquarters. He spoke to his good, retired friend Coady Freeman. "Don't forget us. We'd like for you to come and visit the station someday soon. Oh? You just got a text from John? Is he working at the Sea Fare kitchen today? Is Trish with him? Never mind. Trish just texted me the same thing. Got to go. Take care of yourself, Coady." He hung up the phone as Frank entered his office.

"Lewis and I brought Maho Sato in for questioning. She is in an interrogation room. We haven't kept you as informed as we usually do; so your daughter and Freeman's son are preparing food for the Rotary Club dinner this evening under chef Genzo Yamamoto. Cpl. Lewis and I and your daughter, Trish, and John Freeman landed at the Sea Fare kitchen this morning. All four of us wanted a conversation with a Fuyuki Yoshimurai. We didn't follow RCMP protocol, sir, as Trish and I removed Fuyuki from the kitchen and placed him in an office. We left Cpl. Lewis and John Freeman to investigate the other three caterers through dialogue, Maho, the one we have in custody, Aki Nakamura, and Daigo Suzuki. Trish and I grilled Fuyuki for quite a while until we brought his partner, Maho, into the office with him. She was easier to break down and she explained enough for us to bring her here. We grabbed Fuyuki by the arm and intended to bring him too, but he escaped and now our intention is to keep Maho here to draw Fuyuki out of hiding, sir."

"What does she know and this Fuyuki fellow, is he the lone one who poisoned Ella and Evelyn?"

"We believe that, Rob. And the girl is a decoy to flush Fuyuki out."

"I'm not in agreement with your line of thinking, Frank. If this Fuyuki is our killer, he won't contact his woman at a police station. What have you found out from the girl?"

"She's been with Fuyuki for five years. She was a user and Fuyuki was her dealer. They moved from Tokyo to PEI when they got jobs catering with Genzo's catering service. I was about to make a call to Hiroki Omoto to speak Japanese with her and to help us gain more information through him."

"Don't summon Hiroki just yet. We need a recording of the information you and Trish acquired earlier today. While she is here have her repeat details of this morning's conversation. Find out her address. That would be of a significant advantage in locating your Fuyuki. You can handle this right?"

"Yes. Thank you, Rob." "Then release her."

Trish and John put in a long day preparing for the Rotary Club dinner. Genzo said he was going to bring the food to the Delta Hotel in Charlottetown and set up a buffet table. Aki and Daigo could look after the evening arrangements; so Trish and John were free to go. Trish and John took the Toyota back to Cornwall after being dismissed by Genzo. After Trish dropped John off at his place, she was ready to take a shower and veg out for the evening. Dad was home when she arrived. "How was your day cooking?" asked Dad.

"We were really busy. Genzo is strict. John and I couldn't goof off at all. Did you get any information from Maho? Is she still in a holding cell?"

"Frank questioned her for over an hour. He found out her address; so it's looking as if we can have a stake out surrounding her apartment waiting for Fuyuki to return."

Trish perked up. "A stake out? When and where?

John and I will be there."

"We've got the building under surveillance as we speak. Sgt. Brown and Cpl. Lewis are in an unmarked car at the site. I'm waiting to hear from them. Have you eaten any supper? Take a shower, have a bite and then we'll talk."

Trish turned her exhaustion into excitement as she quickly took a shower and grabbed a sandwich. "I've finished, Dad. Now where is the address?" Rob didn't want to share the information with his daughter, yet he knew how much the mystery club meant to her.

"I can't tell you exactly where the apartment is but I will give you a couple of clues and you can find it for yourself. The Sea Fare kitchen is very near; the Blue Heron Drive can be found; drive to this street and walk around the block. That's all I'm going to say. Keep your cell phone on and take Charlie with you. Be home by eleven."

"Why Charlie? He hasn't been following this case at all. Why not John?"

"Charlie has more experience at night with stake outs. He is older than John and stronger and I feel safer if you've got your brother with you; besides he makes good judgment calls. He's in his room. Tell him to come here and I will break the news to him."

"Charlie, I want you to go with your sister tonight. This is of top priority with the RCMP and it is a stake out. I've given Trish some clues. You'll have to follow her photographic memory and work together. The car must be parked out of sight and you'll have to traipse the rest of the way by foot. Frank and Kurt are already there in an unmarked car. I will not take no for an answer. This is important to Trish and she needs you to calm her down."

"Okay, Dad. I wasn't doing much anyway. It will be like old times, Trish and I going to a stake out. Are you ready to go, Trish?"

"Phone me when you find the place," said Dad. "I'm ready," said Trish. "Let's go."

CHAPTER 14

Charlie drove the car and Trish kept her mind focused. "We have to go back to Stratford, Charlie.

The clues Dad gave me are: go to the Sea Fare kitchen, find Blue Heron Drive, drive down the street, park the car and walk around the block. We should see the unmarked car where Sgt. Brown and Cpl. Lewis are parked. We can do this. We are wearing dark clothes and we've done this before. Are you up for this, Charlie?"

"Yah, Trish. It will be fun."

They were at a disadvantage, as the detectives had weapons and they had none. Nevertheless, Trish was in her element and Charlie was supporting her. They crossed the Hillsborough Bridge and began looking for the Blue Heron Drive once they had spotted the Sea Fare kitchen. Trish spotted it first. "There it is, Charlie; turn left here. Now we drive to the end and park the car."

"Okay, Trish. I'm going to park over there behind the bushes. What's next?"

"We are to walk around the block."

The brother and sister team, like old times, left the car. They moved slowly around the block searching for an apartment building and an unmarked police car. They were surprised to find Frank and Lewis parked several houses down the street spying on a white house with two doors in the front. It was a duplex. They hid behind a row of trees, not wanting the cops to see them. It was 9:00 p.m. and it was dark. By ten they were feeling the October air and it was getting chilly. Shortly after ten they saw a hooded figure walk down the middle of the street, stopping at the white house, looking both ways as if being extra cautious to make a move. The figure couldn't see anyone from his viewpoint and made his way up the steps to the right-hand door of the duplex. "This is it," said Charlie.

"Yes, it's time to make a move."

Simultaneously the four detectives, Brown and Lewis, Trish and Charlie approached the figure and all at once pounced on him. He was dazed. Frank removed the hood and exposed the identity of Daigo! "Where is Fuyuki?" asked Frank.

"What are you doing here?" asked Trish.

Daigo was flabbergasted, "Don't hurt me. Fuyuki texted me to come here after the dinner and I said I would. I don't know where Fuyuki is but he's very mysterious. He may be in Charlottetown or may be at the back door."

The stake out was ruined. "And we all thought he'd be here. Darn it," said Lewis.

"Let's have a moment with Maho," said Trish. Daigo got up and the detectives rang the doorbell. Maho was there in a casual outfit. "Why have you come here? Is Fuyuki with you?"

"We have a search warrant to check your house," said Sgt. Brown.

"We want to check your cell phone," said Charlie. "Where is it?"

Charlie could see it on the coffee table. He grabbed it before Maho had a chance. "I see you've had several texts from Fuyuki today. He told you to stay at home and Daigo would come. This is all true. He also said he'd see you soon at your designated spot at 10:30 p.m. It's almost that time now. Where is that spot, Maho? Time is running out and you must meet him."

"All of us want to find him. You can follow me into the car and take us to him," said Frank who grabbed her arm and led her to the car. Everyone else left the house including Daigo. The duplex was empty. The detectives were on a wild-goose chase with Maho giving them explicit instructions on how to get to Fuyuki. Trish and Charlie walked back to the old Toyota. Daigo disappeared into the darkness down the street and around the corner.

Trish was exceptionally intuitive. Her premonitions overwhelmed her. "Charlie, don't drive away. I think Daigo was a decoy for Fuyuki to get into the house. Maho is taking the detectives on a fictitious hunt. I think Fuyuki has gone back to the duplex. Let's text Dad and say we will be detained and not to worry about us. Then let's head back to Maho's house."

"I'll text Dad," said Charlie.

In minutes the two young detectives headed back to the duplex. They didn't go to the front door but maneuvered towards the back doorway. The back door was unlocked. Silently they crept into the kitchen of the duplex and found Fuyuki lying on the couch in the living room. Charlie and Trish took him by surprise and instantly Charlie put him in an arm hold. Trish called 911 and Dad. Fuyuki was strong but Charlie was stronger. It was a good thing that Trish had brought rope with them; they tied Fuyuki to a chair and waited for an RCMP vehicle to arrive. Quickly a vehicle reached the house and an officer put Fuyuki in handcuffs and escorted him to the police car.

Frank and Lewis realized Maho was leading them astray. They gave up listening to her directions, ignored her instructions, and headed back to the duplex. They arrived to find out that an RCMP police vehicle was in the driveway and Fuyuki was handcuffed and in the back seat of the car. They also noticed Trish and Charlie Camden were there and about to leave. "Those two Camden's seem to be in the middle every time," said Frank.

CHAPTER 15

Fuyuki was now in custody and was placed in a holding cell until he could be interrogated by the detectives in the morning. Trish and Charlie were home by 11:30 p.m.

It had been quite a night. Trish's premonitions could always be counted upon.

The interrogation of Fuyuki was no better the morning after his arrest. Sgt. Brown tried to crack his resolve until finally Fuyuki said, "I want a lawyer."

"You may call one now," said Frank.

Fuyuki called Thomas Stretch who said to him, "Don't say a word until I get there."

Trish wanted to visit the RCMP station but Dad said to leave it in the hands of the detectives and legal system; so she decided to visit Hiroki and Akiko. She texted John and he said he would meet her there. Hiroki answered the door and the two young detectives were welcomed inside. Once they were settled in the living room, Trish told them that the RCMP had a Fuyuki in custody and he was very stubborn and not speaking to anyone. Hiroki pondered whether this Fuyuki was the same one who had lost all his investments through Hiroki's business deals. He said, "How can I find out if this is the same Fuyuki who made an investment in my business back in Japan and lost all his money? This is motive for his hatred that would lead him to kill my daughter. I'd like to go to the headquarters and find out for myself. Will you come with me, Trish and John?"

"Dad told me not to go but I've never kept that from my trying to solve a crime. John, will you come too?" asked Trish.

"Let's go," said John.

Akiko stayed home while Hiroki, Trish, and John left for the station. They arrived to find out that the lawyer Fuyuki hired was the same one from the last case, Thomas Stretch, a sleazy lawyer who had connections with the Mafia. Rob was miffed that Trish and John showed up at the RCMP station but didn't send them home. Instead they accompanied Frank and Lewis with Hiroki to the room with the two-way mirror. They couldn't hear the conversation between Stretch and Fuyuki but it was recorded as they spoke.

"What is your predicament?" asked Thomas. "The Yakuza in Japan said they would set me free if I did one last job for them, to kill Hiroki's daughter." "Why?"

"They were very envious of the empire of wealth that Hiroki had and they wanted him to experience pain. I, too, had my personal anger at Hiroki for the loss of money I had invested in his business. I blamed Hiroki for that loss."

"So, that's it," said Stretch. "You killed Hiroki's daughter?"

"I wanted to remain clean and start a new life here in PEI but I had this one last job to do to get a free start from the Yakuza. I knew Ayumi could eat only gluten-free foods which was told to me back home and when Genzo made gluten-free brownies, I could not bring myself to poison her. I did not kill Hiroki's daughter. By accident one other person ate one and also died.

Hiroki, a mild Japanese man became hysterical. He ran out of the room he was in and charged into the middle of the testimony Fuyuki was giving to Thomas. He grabbed Fuyuki around the neck and began choking him. "You killed my only daughter! You killed Ayumi! You lost your investments because you didn't show any interest in the stock market. That is not my fault. You work for the Yakuza!"

Pandemonium quickly followed. The detectives forced Hiroki to release Fuyuki and shoved him out of the room. Thomas Stretch sat calmly at the table while all this was happening around him. Trish and John continued to view the scene through the two-way mirror. Frank and Lewis proceeded to regain some sense of order in the room. They had it on record that Fuyuki was not guilty or so he said. Fuyuki knew better than to try to escape. Nevertheless he was unnerved by Hiroki's attack.

Hiroki was sent to a holding cell where he broke down in sobs and wails of emotion.

Fuyuki was back in the room with Thomas. Now was the time, thought Stretch, to really get some testimony from his client without the audio tape.

Fuyuki said, "the Yakuza or you call it the Mafia have a world-wide network. I was promised that this one last job would set me free. I want to live without the Yakuza controlling my life. Can you help set me free?"

"Since we are off the record, there are only two things I can do for you. You must have a hearing about the charge of murder which will end up in court. I will defend you. Secondly, I can send you away from PEI to a remote place with a new identity."

"Can I take my partner, Maho, with me?" "No. This is only a one-person offer."

"I cannot leave Maho behind. I will face the judge," said Fuyuki.

"Very well," said Thomas, "I'll prepare you for a court hearing and the inevitable court trial."

Meanwhile Hiroki was subdued and more in control of himself. Rob Camden knew of his friendship with Trish; so he told him to go home, as there was nothing he could do and he wouldn't be charged with aggravated assault. Hiroki bowed to Rob and said, "You are a good man. I thank you for not charging me for my outburst. I will go home now."

Rob also spoke to Trish and John so that they could get a ride home with Hiroki, as they came with him and they had no other way home. They had to leave the RCMP headquarters. They then left with Hiroki.

Frank and Kurt didn't have a confession on tape. However they knew he was guilty. Fuyuki would be staying in a holding cell until the hearing and then he'd be kept at Sleepy Hollow jail until the trial. Thomas Stretch was finished with Fuyuki for now. He had work to do in preparation for his case.

"We've won the first round, haven't we?" said Lewis.

"Maybe the first round but not the final one," said Frank. "I don't trust that lawyer. He slipped one by us the last time and I'm not too sure he might do it again."

CHAPTER 16

Thomas Stretch was in touch with Gondola, the Mafia head of all of Canada, who lived in Toronto.

Stretch prepared for a jury that consisted of twelve members. He didn't want to lose this case; however, he intended to find a jury of his own, either by blackmail, threats, or by coercion. Gondola supported Stretch by providing him with a list of names and a corrupt judge who could be easily coerced. What Thomas didn't know was the name of the prosecutor.

At the initial hearing there was no jury and Thomas said that Fuyuki should plead not guilty. He was sentenced to be sent to Sleepy Hollow jail until the court trial. This gave Stretch just enough time to get his blackmailed jury in place.

The Justice Department hired a prosecutor for the trial.

Trish was at home and school which kept her life in order but she continued to hound her dad for details as to when the trial was to take place. She kept in contact with Hiroki and Akiko, and the mystery club members. She decided to have a meeting of the CMC to share any news they had for the trial. Josie and John arrived, and Paul was late as usual, with coffee in one hand and chips in the other. Charlie decided to pay a visit to the club members.

Trish said, "I open this meeting to share the news or lack of news about the condition our criminal is in as well as an update on the Omoto's, Maho, and Genzo and the catering group. As you know from our texts, Fuyuki is at Sleepy Hollow jail waiting for a court date. He pleaded not guilty to the murder of Ella which leads me to the state of the Omoto's. They are very sad and lonely and I thought it would be a good idea if we took turns to visit them or brought them things to cheer them up. It takes time to overcome grief but we can share our stories with them and memories of their daughter. How does everyone feel about that?"

"I think it's a good idea," said Josie. The rest said they agreed.

"Maho is working for Genzo again and the catering service is doing quite well. Genzo hired another Japanese man to help cook in Fuyuki's place. I overheard a conversation Dad had with Sgt. Brown saying the trial would be soon. The corrupt lawyer, Thomas Stretch, has been trying to exert his influence on jury members for the trial."

Charlie said, "Thomas Stretch pulled a fast one when Rufus MacInnis disappeared. He's likely to create havoc with the jury even though he won't be allowed to choose all twelve members. He will blackmail several, I'm sure of that."

"When the time comes, will our club be allowed to attend the trial?" asked Paul.

"That's a good question. I know we've attended before; so we'll have to get approval from our dad. He's not going to approve our missing school to attend, I'm sure of that," said Trish. The meeting was adjourned and they all wondered about the outcome of the trial and who the prosecutor would be.

Frank and Lewis had a matched fingerprint of Fuyuki on the syringe with the one they took at the RCMP station before he was sent to Sleepy Hollow. The evidence was conclusive. They had a date for the trial which was to start on Monday, January 15.

The Camden Club had school and the members were not permitted to attend. The jury was in place. The prosecutor was MacKenzie Pathius, Mack Pathius' brother. Thomas Stretch was dressed in a suit and tie. Fuyuki Yoshimurai was presentable in a clean shirt, sweater, and dress pants. The audience consisted of Coady Freeman, Hiroki Omoto, Rob Camden, Maho Sato, Dan Redmond and several others unknown as to their connection. The clerk of the court came in and asked everyone to rise while the judge appeared from a side door. The judge was Cameron Hinkle. He told everyone to sit and the trial would begin.

This was a first for Fuyuki. He was nervous. Thomas was in his element. He knew most of the jury and Judge Hinkle. He didn't know the prosecutor, MacKenzie Pathius, but he had heard of him.

The evidence was clear even though Fuyuki pleaded not guilty. The prosecutor in addition to wanting a guilty plea for Fuyuki was determined to find out the source of the fentanyl that Fuyuki obtained. He was like a dog with a bone when Fuyuki took the stand. "You say you are not guilty of injecting fentanyl into the gluten-free brownies, yet we have evidence that your fingerprint was on the syringe found at the Confederation Mall kitchen. What we don't know is the name of the person you bought the fentanyl from here in Prince Edward Island. Now, speak up and tell us who it is?"

"The Yakuza will kill me if I disclose the source," said Fuyuki nervously.

MacKenzie said, "You have no choice. You either disclose the drug dealer's name or you go to prison."

Fuyuki said, "I will not give out this information."

MacKenzie spoke to the jury and they decided to go into closed quarters to decide Fuyuki's fate. Thomas Stretch was confident with the jury. When the jury returned, Judge Hinkle asked for the verdict.

"A verdict couldn't be reached. We didn't all agree."

MacKenzie was angry. He said, "The evidence is obvious."

Stretch just smiled.

"We will have to conclude that this is a mistrial and we have no reason to keep Fuyuki in jail. He is free to leave."

Rob and Coady were disgusted. Hiroki was horrified at the lack of justice in the province. Maho was delighted and got up and came forward to wrap her arms around her partner. Dan Redmond was despondent over the whole process. The trial was over.

Fuyuki bowed to Thomas Stretch and thanked him. He knew he was a free man. The Yakuza wouldn't touch him now. He had kept their secret of the identity of the drug dealer.

Back at the office Rob texted his daughter on her lunch break. "It was a mistrial. Fuyuki is free."

Trish texted the club about the news. They were very disappointed but nevertheless decided to have a CMC meeting that night.

The CMC all came together in the cozy basement of the Camden home. It didn't feel like a party. They shared their frustrations and disillusionment about the justice system. They had nothing good to say about Thomas Stretch. They all decided to go over to Hiroki and Akiko's as a group to share their grief.

They were welcomed. Hiroki thanked them for their visit and asked them to please drop in any time.

Rob talked to Trish when she got home. "Well Trish, justice doesn't always work in this world."

She hugged her dad and started to cry.

CHAPTER 17

Six months later, Hiroki still couldn't get over the death of his only daughter. Akiko continued to grieve too. Both had their ways of dealing with their grief and neither spoke of it to each other. Trish suffered her own grief in dealing with her friend's murder. It wasn't fair and the legal system let them down.

Rob Camden became a significant person in Hiroki's life. Rob said to Hiroki that it was possible to have a new trial. Hiroki went to the Department of Justice for Prince Edward Island and made a request for another judge who would pick a new jury to take over the case. It was one of those things Hiroki felt driven to do. He couldn't bring Ayumi back but he would hopefully have the satisfaction of putting Fuyuki where he belonged. The Justice Department agreed with his request because of the significant evidence. A new judge, by the name of Harold Campbell, was assigned to the court for a new trial. Harold Campbell would pick his own jury.

Hiroki was pleased that he, at the very least, could foresee justice with the Thomas Stretch fiasco. Rob came home to tell

Trish that a new trial would be held. "Dad, that's the best news I've heard about Ella's case in a long time."

Fuyuki was informed that he was to be tried again with a new judge. He had to find a new lawyer. Maho was worried. Things had not been going well for them lately and they were struggling financially. Fuyuki asked Genzo for the name of a new lawyer and Genzo said his lawyer was Ikko Suzuki. Fuyuki made arrangements to meet this person.

The trial date was set. Trish and the CMC were allowed to come to the trial, as it wasn't on a school day. Harold Campbell had his jury in place. Fuyuki was seated with his new lawyer, Ikko Suzuki. MacKenzie Pathius was the crown prosecutor. The evidence was put forth. The finger print on the syringe and Fuyuki's fingerprint taken at the RCMP office were an exact match. The jury's verdict was unanimous. Fuyuki was guilty. Harold Campbell sentenced him to twenty years in the Atlantic Prison in Renous, New Brunswick. It was a maximum-security prison.

Hiroki was satisfied. There was finally justice in Prince Edward Island. The mystery club was also content with the verdict. Maho made a decision right there in the chambers to go home to her parents in Tokyo. She was worried about their acceptance of her after such a long time; however, she needed to rebuild her relationship with them. She no longer was a user. She was clean and maybe she could take a course to educate herself.

The Camden Mystery Club had their standard end- of-case party. They all congregated in the basement of the Camden house to celebrate the restoration of justice. What happened to Thomas Stretch? He was disbarred and left PEI and moved to Toronto to assist Gondola. There will always be evil in the world but justice prevails almost all of the time.